_July 2017_

# A Bolt Hole for Zelda

_To Linda_

D1809699

## By

## Amanda M Arnold

_Best Wishes_
_Amanda M Arnold._

## A modern saga of Cornwall

After living a life in the Home Counties, Zelda flees a failing relationship to a new life in Cornwall. New friends, a new romance, and discovering the mysteries of her past, means that her life takes many twists and turns before everything is finally explained, and she eventually finds happiness.

**Published by and available from**
The Endless Bookcase Ltd
71 Castle Road, St Albans, Hertfordshire,
England, UK, AL1 5DQ
www.theendlessbookcase.com

**Printed Edition**
Also available in multiple e-book formats via The Endless
Bookcase website, Amazon, Kobo and Nook.

**Printed in the United Kingdom**
First Printing, 2017

**ISBN: 978-1-908941-92-3**

# Acknowledgement

A special thanks to Georgina for her invaluable help and support.

# About the author

Amanda M Arnold grew up in London and worked in the fashion world. She is married with two grown up sons and has lived in Norfolk and Essex. Now retired, Amanda lives in the countryside and her interests include: art, entertaining, birdwatching and films. She also belongs to a local creative writing group. Amanda has travelled widely and is a keen photographer.

# CHAPTER 1
## ESCAPE

Zelda was doing a runner. She loaded the car with the things she loved best, her two dogs, Henry and Prince, and her favourite clothes and photos in a large suitcase. The remaining available space was filled with potted plants, cookery books and some framed pictures, plus the dogs' bowls, their beds, and cheese sandwiches for her to eat on the journey.

She locked the front door and had a last look at the magnificent Victorian house she was leaving forever. Then climbing into the car, she drove off not glancing at the flowerbeds that she had tended so carefully for eight long years.

The note on the kitchen table would explain to Donald her reasons for leaving when he returned from New York that evening. It was hard to put into words that what had once been thrilling and exciting was now just sad and boring. Her birthday, two days ago which had passed without even a phone call or card from him, had made up her mind and the visit from the solicitor yesterday had done the rest.

On a long stretch of featureless straight road, it began to rain. The windscreen wipers swished from side to side and Zelda's thoughts returned to the start of her romance with Donald.

It had been a stifling hot evening in New York and as the recently promoted personal assistant, this was the first time she had accompanied him on a business trip.

They had met up with a new client at a Greenwich Village restaurant. After a couple of stiff Martinis, Zelda relaxed and enjoyed the meal and the great atmosphere. Donald was amusing and the conversation drifted from holidays to business, seamlessly. Leaving the restaurant and saying goodbye to the client, Donald hailed a cab to take them back to their hotel near Times Square.

'Did you enjoy that?' he queried. 'New York is my favourite place; it has such a raw energy.'

Zelda smiled at him happily. 'Yes it's my first time here and I can see why people love it.'

Passing a still open bookshop Donald asked the cab driver to stop. 'We will walk from here.' he said.

The driver turned to look over his shoulder. 'OK folks, but be careful.'

Donald helped Zelda out of the cab and passed the driver several dollar bills.

'I need a book to help me wind down after work, even if it has been with pleasant company my mind is still buzzing,' he said by way of explanation.

Zelda could not believe that shops were still open as it was nearly midnight. After Donald had bought a bestselling novel and a magazine for Zelda, they strolled down Fifth Avenue, passing a photo shoot on the steps of a church, where a beautiful girl and a male model, stood posing as a bridal couple. Further on, a string quartet, the musicians dressed in evening suits, played on the sidewalk collecting money from passers-by.

When they reached their hotel and were going up in the lift Zelda sneaked a furtive look at Donald. As her employer, she had not taken much of a personal interest in him before. Now in the mirrored lift she could see he was handsome in an ultra; smooth way. He obviously worked out and there were no wrinkles in his perfectly tailored suit. His eyes were a grey-blue, depending on the light and his wavy hair a warm brown.

She flushed as he turned suddenly and caught her stare. Luckily, they had reached their floor and Donald stood back to allow her to leave the lift first

Outside the door of Zelda's room Donald watched her put the key card in the lock but it didn't open. 'Here let me,' he said and the door swung open at his first try. 'Girls and mechanical things,' he said, his laugh was warm and sexy. It was the first personal moment they had ever had.

'Darling does it have to end here?' Donald's voice was soft as he took a step into the room to hold the door open for her.

Zelda felt her pulse race as she weighed up the situation. 'Perhaps you won't need your book after all,' she said quietly following him inside and closing the door.

There was hooting from the car behind and Zelda realised she had driven slower and slower as she relived that first night.

'Sorry. 'She said out loud and waved hoping the driver behind could see her through the back window. 'Must concentrate,' she murmured knowing no one could hear her.

Only stopping to let the dogs out a couple of times she arrived in the Cornish village and eventually found Marryat House about a few hundred yards beyond the row of fishermen's cottages.

It was pitch black but by the light of her torch, she made out the name on the garden gate, which swung open with a grating squeak when she lifted the latch. Flashing her torch round she saw the outline of the house and a garage on the left hand side with a shingle drive leading up to it. No gate, just a gap in the front wall. Parking the car, she let the dogs out, more for a feeling of protection and support, then followed the beam of the torch over what might have been a lawn, but was now just knee high grass. There was a porch with different coloured panes of glass to the sides and door.

In her pocket were the two keys that the solicitor had given her along with the deeds to the house. The keys were attached to a buff coloured label with Marryat House written on it in rather smudged ink. The first one fitted and after a short tussle with the lock, the door opened. Zelda's feet crunched on a pile of mail as she walked hesitantly into the porch. A huge cobweb wrapped itself around her face, she shuddered and stifled a scream.

'That's it boys,' she said to the dogs, 'we'll wait until the morning.'

Back at the car she took out the two dog bowls and filled them from the remaining bottle of water, leaving just enough for her to drink. Then with the dogs on the back seat, she sat in the driver's seat and finished the sandwiches, snuggled down under her coat, and fell fast asleep.

She awoke to see a face peering in the car window and the dogs growling.

'Sorry, I didn't mean to startle you, are you OK?' said a blonde girl about her own age. 'I was passing and thought you might have been taken ill. I am Jenny the local Doctors' practice nurse so it could have been an early call.'

Zelda struggled upright and opened the car door.

'Thanks for asking but I'm fine. We arrived too late to go into the house last night so I thought I'd wait for daylight.'

Jenny smiled. 'I don't blame you the house has been empty since poor Tommy......' her voice trailed away not wanting to go into details. 'Well as there are no problems I better go or I'll be late for work.'

Zelda was wide-awake now and realised Jenny could fill in the background to many of her questions.

'When I have settled in will you come round for a cup of coffee and a chat?'

'I'd like that. I live in the last of the cottages down the hill so it's no distance to walk,' and with a cheery wave, Jenny strode away.

The second key opened the front door and Zelda edged slowly into the hall. There was a staircase to her right with a couple of bends in it before it reached the upstairs. She opened the first door on the left hand side of the hall, which revealed a dining room with a large oval table and six chairs, a sideboard and a cabinet containing glasses and decanters. The next door opened into a light and airy sitting room with French doors leading to the garden. The three-piece suite had seen better days and the loose covers were of a 1930's swirly design. However, the large television was right up to the minute. There was a film of dust over everything, but it was not as bad as she had anticipated. Ahead was the kitchen, but before tackling that Zelda was curious to explore the bedrooms.

Telling the dogs to stay, she climbed the stairs. There were three good sized bedrooms, a large bathroom and separate toilet. Between the bathroom and a bedroom, there was another door that she took to be a storage cupboard. No time to investigate now, the kitchen was her priority.

Downstairs the dogs were sitting staring at the kitchen, no doubt hoping it contained food. 'OK boys,' Zelda laughed, 'let's sort you out.'

With that, she went to the car and came back with their two beds, which fitted nicely in the space before the stairs along with their bowls and tins of food.

The dogs fed, she realised that without a hot drink she could not tackle what lay ahead. The solicitor had said that all the services had been left on so it was time to find out if that was the case.

Having run the taps for a while, Zelda rinsed out and filled the kettle, then put it on the cooker. The burner lit first time and soon the water was boiling away. Rooting round the pantry, she found a jar of instant coffee. Luckily, she could drink coffee without milk, so she found a mug with a red and black design round the base and put a good teaspoon of coffee in it, then stirred in the boiling water. Soon she was ready to begin the big clean up.

In a tall cupboard in the kitchen Zelda discovered a fully working Hoover, and under the sink a selection of sprays and polishes. Tommy was no slouch at keeping things clean, or did he have a cleaning lady? So many questions but as yet no answers. Shooing the dogs into the garden and flinging open all the windows she set to work. It was late afternoon before all the rooms had been cleaned to her satisfaction, the bedding in the front bedroom had been washed, tumble-dried, and the bed remade. Tonight she would sleep in a bed in her own house, but first there was a pressing need to get supplies before the shops closed.

The dogs bounded on to the back seats of the car and sat with their noses out of the half opened windows, one each side. Zelda drove past the cottages on the right hand side and the curving bay on the left, and they soon arrived in the village. By the Anchor pub, there were several shops, so Zelda stopped the car and parked by the double fronted general store. Leaving the dogs in the car, she picked up a wire basket from a pile by the front door and went in. The store was well stocked and soon she had all the basics she needed, plus cans of dog food.

'Have you dog biscuits?' Zelda asked the young man at the till, 'I need a large bag, I have two big, hungry dogs to feed.'

The young man smiled and nodded then disappeared into the back of the shop and returned with a large sack of dog biscuits. 'Will this do?' He enquired.

'Thank you that is just the job.' Zelda said paying him.

Then while trying to carry all the bags she dropped the dog biscuits and her purse. A man in dark blue overalls who had been looking in the frozen food cabinet stepped forward and picked them up.

'Here let me help you to your car,' he said. 'I saw your two dogs in it when I came in, lovely Red Setters aren't they?'

Zelda nodded. 'Yes they are my best buddies. Thank you that would be such a help.'

At the car, he loaded all the shopping into the boot. 'I haven't seen you round here before, where are you staying?' he said.

'I've just moved into Marryat House.' Zelda replied.

'What Tommy Tree's old place? I used to go there when his car was on the blink. My name is Joe, I run the local petrol station and car maintenance centre. Is the car still there?'

Zelda looked surprised. 'I really don't know. There has been so much to do today I have not even looked in the garage yet, but I shall go back now and check. What sort of car was it?'

Joe closed the boot of the car. 'An original orange MGB. Tommy really loved that car, perhaps not the best car for round these parts in the winter, but in the summer with the roof open it was perfect.'

Zelda would have liked to ask more about Tommy, the few details she had were sketchy, but that would have to wait for now.

'Thanks for your help Joe, I expect I shall see you again soon,' and with a friendly wave she started the engine and drove off.

The double wooden doors of the garage were locked. Zelda stared at them trying to think where the key might be. Then she remembered seeing a bunch of keys hanging on a nail by the kitchen door. Entering the house, she ran to the kitchen and there they were, some rusty, some shiny, but which one? With the dogs watching Zelda first tried the shiny ones, thinking that they must be the most used. The fourth one turned in the lock, the door swung open and there it was, a beautiful orange MGB. Zelda caught her breath. 'Wow' she breathed, 'thank you Tommy, I will look after it.'

For several minutes she stood transfixed, then jolting back to reality, she locked the garage doors and calling the dogs, unloaded the shopping and went inside. Looking down at their puzzled faces Zelda laughed and said. 'That's it boys, we're home.'

# CHAPTER 2
## SETTLING IN

Next morning dawned bright and clear. Zelda opened her eyes and wondered for a short moment where she was, then as the light streamed through the half closed curtains, she remembered the events of the last few days. Great! she thought, time to explore and then I will tackle the garden.

Pulling on her jeans and a thick jumper, she went downstairs to be greeted by Henry and Prince, tails wagging and both standing by the front door making it plain that a walk was what they wanted. Outside, Zelda crossed the road and stood looking over the cliff-top at the bay below. A great curve of pale yellow sand, and the sparkling blue sea, stretching out to the horizon met her gaze. There was a rough path down to the beach with a wooden handrail and steps for the last few feet. The dogs ran ahead and were soon on the sand, chasing each other, their ears streaming behind them in the breeze. Zelda followed, breathing in the lovely salty air. I'm going to like this place, she thought. Further up the beach was a man with a camera, taking photos. The dogs bounded up to him.

'Prince, Henry, come here,' Zelda called, eventually catching up with them.

The man laughed. 'Great names. Who are you Queen Anne?' He was tall and sun tanned with dark hair and twinkling blue eyes.

'Sorry about my dogs, it's our first walk here and they're a bit excited. No, I'm Zelda and those were their names when I bought them from the kennels. Their father was called King, hence the royal connection.'

The man nodded, 'Ah that explains it. I'm taking photo shots and doing link shots for a TV programme about Cornwall. This is a great place, which I have discovered has a history of smuggling.'

Zelda shook her head. 'I really don't know much about the area yet, we only arrived yesterday.'

The man bent down and patted the dogs then smiled up at Zelda, 'That's fine, have a good walk. By the way, my name is Harrison. Perhaps I will bump into you again, I hope so.'

Zelda looked at his retreating back as he strode off. I hope so too, she thought.

Crossing the road on the way back, Zelda glanced over at the house, something struck her as odd. What was it? Then she realised, there was a room built over the garage. Puzzled, when she was back inside she ran up the stairs and tried to think how to get into it, then noticed the door she had thought was a cupboard. It opened revealing a long, narrow room in a very untidy state. There were unfinished canvases lined up against the walls, a big colourful abstract painting on an easel and paint splashes all over the bare wooden floor. Tommy had obviously dabbled at painting. Was it a hobby or did he sell them? Two guitars hung on the wall above a workbench on which were all manner of art materials, pots of paint, brushes stuck in jam jars, pencils and a collection of sketches of sea birds. They were very good. Also underneath were various magazines.

Zelda glanced round the room and realised there was a shower room at the rear and a small kitchenette with a window that overlooked the back garden. A previous owner must have added this on as a granny flat. The kitchenette contained a fridge, washing machine, a microwave and an electric kettle, what a find. Zelda wandered over to the pile of magazines, drawn by an unexplained feeling that there was something important in them. The top one was a year old and opened at the page that showed photos of people in the business world at a fund raising event. A circle had been drawn in biro round a smiling couple. It was of her and Donald. The blurb under the photo read, "Mr Donald Ferguson and his fiancée, Zelda arriving at a Mayfair charity launch, sponsored by the D F Hedge Fund."

'Eureka,' Zelda said aloud, 'now I know how Tommy found me.'

Downstairs, she opened the backdoor and followed by the dogs stepped into the garden. At first, she was appalled by the sad state of neglect that met her gaze. Paths were overgrown by trailing climbers that had nowhere to climb, dead flowers obliterated what could have been raised beds, towards the far end was a large pond choked with weeds and dead lilies, fruit trees bent with unpicked, rotting fruit. Standing there with the warm sun on her face Zelda suddenly felt a surge of happiness. I'll make this lovely again, she thought, I'll sit on that old oak bench with a cup of coffee and view a perfect scene. Then she sighed, thinking of the work she had to do before that could happen.

'Rome wasn't built in a day and I have lots of time,' she muttered, half to herself and half to the dogs who had come back after scampering excitedly round their new territory.

Running along the entire back of the house was a crazy paving patio. Tobacco plants grew up between the cracks but that was OK, it was in keeping with the rustic feel of the garden. Zelda went to the car and unloaded the potted plants she had brought with her, they were a bit droopy but she found a watering can in the garden shed and filled it from the water butt that stood outside the back door. They'd soon perk up she thought. Next, she had a good look in the shed. A large sit on lawn mower nearly filled it. 'What fun' Zelda said aloud.

When she had lived with Donald, they had the same type of mower, which only the gardener used but now she would sit on this one and cut the grass herself. However, there were still more things to look at, on the other side of the house to the garage was a large conservatory.

Zelda found the door unlocked, opened it and went inside. There were several broken panes of glass but otherwise it was in a good state. It would be lovely in the winter as it caught the morning sun. Next, she unloaded the rest of her possessions from the car. Having already cleaned the inside of the wardrobe and chest of drawers, she unpacked her clothes and the contents of the suitcase.

When she came to the two silver framed photos, one of her mother and the other of her Grandmother, Zelda put them on the top of the dressing table, then sat on the end of the bed and stared at them, what would they think now if they were still around? They had both had their share of tragedy as well as good times, but had always kept their sense of humour and resourcefulness, come what may.

Her mother's short life had established her as a star of screen and stage, while her Grandmother had blazed the trail of the super models. By comparison, her job as a PA, lacked the excitement of the fashion and film world; however, it had led to her working for Donald and becoming his fiancée. Their life together had been fun at the beginning. Zelda had enjoyed the lavish entertaining at their home, or playing hostess on a yacht rented for the Cannes film festival, also the numerous holidays they had in exotic places. On reflection, Zelda realised that lifestyle had not been real, in the sense that making Marryat House a proper home would be, because that would all be down to her.

By now, it was past midday and the sun was high in the sky, what a great time to try out the MG Zelda thought, going for the fun option. The car has been stationary for a while so may not start she thought, excusing herself from the prospect of a stint in the garden, that would have to wait. Finding the keys on the kitchen worktop and leaving the dogs in the garden, Zelda opened the garage doors and sat in the driver's seat. To her delight the engine fired into life at the first try, obviously Joe had done a good maintenance job. After backing out, she drove along the coast road delighting in the husky roar of the engine. When she came to the Anchor pub, she turned in and parked. It was quite busy inside with several men leaning on the bar, and three couples sitting, eating at tables. Zelda studied the blackboard with its chalky written menu, offering local caught fish and various other options. 'Can I have the baked potato with tuna and salad?' She said to the girl behind the bar.

The girl nodded 'Anything to drink?' She asked looking at Zelda curiously.

'Just a tonic, lemon and ice please, I'm driving so that will be all thanks.' Zelda paid and took her drink over to a table by the window.

A tall man with his dark, thick hair tied back in a ponytail was staring at her and finally came over to her table. 'Excuse me for bothering you, but I saw you arrive, isn't that Tommy's MGB you were driving?'

What a small bubble this place is Zelda thought, everyone knows everyone's business, and if they don't, they ask. However, she smiled up at him and said, 'yes that is right, did you know Tommy?'

He held out his hand and shook hers. 'I am Cador, I used to help him with his garden. Tommy had no idea about gardens, so as I run a market garden and landscaping business with my brother, I was up there quite a lot.'

He gave Zelda a flashing smile showing a row of gleaming white teeth, and she noticed that as he smiled his dark brown eyes glinted like coal in the beam of a flashlight. 'Wonderful,' Zelda replied, 'perhaps you could do the same for me? I'm afraid the garden is all overgrown and needs a lot of attention. When could you start?'

Cador pulled out a mobile phone and scanned it intently. 'I could start tomorrow. I have a couple of days clear before we start another project.'

The girl from behind the bar came up with Zelda's order.

Cador gave another one of his smiles. 'I'll leave you to enjoy your meal then, until tomorrow.' With that, he turned on his heel and went back to his place at the bar.

The girl stared after him with obvious warmth, then bent down and whispered in Zelda's ear, 'Watch out for him, he's dynamite, all the girls are after him.'

Zelda laughed. 'Not this girl, I just want someone to do my garden.'

The food was excellent, and when she had finished, Zelda got up from the table, and smiling at several faces turned toward her, she left the Anchor and drove back along the coast road.

# CHAPTER 3
# PROGRESS

As Zelda was driving past the cottages, she spotted Jenny, pliers in hand, cutting dead roses and putting them in an overflowing wicker flower trug. Pulling up, she called out. 'Hi Jenny, how about coming for coffee tomorrow morning?'

Jenny straightened up and pushing her long blonde hair back from her face, she smiled in recognition. 'Zelda, yes I have a free day, so that would be lovely, ten thirty OK?'

'Fine, see you tomorrow, bye.' Zelda waved and drove back to Marryat House thinking perhaps soon, I will learn more about Tommy and how we are connected.

Back at the house the dogs were pleased to see her, and once she let them in they ran to the front door obviously wanting a walk. It was a lovely warm afternoon so it was a good time to explore some more. The tide was out, and now she could see that there were large rocks to the left hand side of the beach. Clambering over them and rounding the corner Zelda saw there was a small cove that could only be reached at low tide. Sea birds wheeled overhead, their shrill calls filled the air and stopped when they landed on their nests, dotted along the cliff. It was a lovely hidden cove. Was this the old smugglers haunt that Harrison had referred to the other morning?

The dogs bounded happily about at the water's edge, Zelda kicked off her shoes and paddled into the sea, it was a bit cold to start with but she stood and wiggled her toes, sinking slowly into the sand and after a while, the water felt quite warm. Prince came running up with a large piece of driftwood in his mouth, taking it from him Zelda threw it into the sea and laughed as he and Henry rushed to see who would reach it first and bring it back to her. Eventually tiring of the game, she picked up her shoes and calling the dogs walked barefoot back over the rocks and up the path. 'I am going native,' she said, aloud, with a chuckle.

The rest of the day passed quickly as she thoroughly cleaned the kitchen and utility room, filling the dishwasher, first with all the crockery and cutlery and then with pots and pans. If I'm entertaining, Zelda thought I want everything perfect, even if it is just for a cup of coffee. In the utility room, she noticed there was a door into the conservatory, it was locked from the inside but the key was in the lock. I must ask Cador who round here replaces broken windowpanes, then I can make full use of the conservatory. Suddenly she realised it was getting dark, so after feeding the dogs she made a cheese sandwich and settled in front of the TV. It was the usual mix of quite good dramas and ghastly reality programs, in which everyone seemed permanently in tears. What had happened to people?

'Man up,' she shouted at the screen. Then laughed thinking gosh, living alone I'm getting like a mad old maid and I've only been here three days.

Bored with the television Zelda thought, why waste time, I wonder if there are any clues up in the studio that could solve the mystery of who Tommy had been. Opening the door and switching on the light the smell of paint was quite overpowering. Going over to where the piles of pictures leant against the wall, Zelda started to flick through them. There were many landscapes, none of which looked as if they were of local places, more like scenes of a warmer, and far distant land. The next pile contained portraits, mainly of girls although there were some of very arty looking men with long hair and musical instruments. Zelda gazed up at the two guitars on the wall, they did look well used and very expensive. Had Tommy been an aspiring musician as well as an artist? Rifling through a third pile she came to a portrait of a very pretty girl with long blonde hair and slanting green eyes. The girl looked familiar. Suddenly she realised the identity of the girl; it was Jenny.

# CHAPTER 4
## JENNY

Exactly at ten thirty, Jenny arrived.

'Come in', Zelda said, 'do you mind sitting in the kitchen? I have Cador working in the garden and I want to keep an eye out in case he wants to ask me a question.'

Jenny laughed, 'I know what that question will be, he has quite a reputation you know.'

Zelda shook her head. 'I am only interested in him making the garden lovely again, nothing else.'

She handed Jenny a mug of coffee and sitting down opposite her at the table, smiled in a 'tell me more kind of way.'

Jenny stared round the kitchen. 'I often came to the house when Tommy lived here, so I know it really well. Tommy painted a couple of pictures of me. I have one hanging over the mantelpiece in my house. He was a terrific artist and told me he had trained at the Slade School of Fine Art when he was a teenager. Of course that was before he went to America.'

'Do you know why he went there?' Zelda asked feeling that at last she was finding some sense to this mystery.

'Well, he said that while he was at the Slade he had formed a rock group with three other boys and they had been discovered by an agent who offered them a two-year tour of the States. They had an instant success out there and continued touring for years. Eventually, interest dwindled and the group broke up, but Tommy settled in California, in Bolinas where many musicians and some artists live.'

Zelda smiled at her. 'That's great! at least I can begin to get a handle on who Tommy was and what made him tick'.

'Do you mean you never met Tommy and yet he left you this house?' Jenny said incredulously.

Zelda nodded. 'I know it's amazing, but I expect he thought he would be here for a long time. Please tell me what happened.'

Before Jenny could answer there was a knock on the back door. Zelda opened the door and Cador stood there, sweat ran down his face, while his bare arms displayed a couple of recent tattoos.

'I'm sorry to bother you Zelda, but before I can use the lawn mower, I'll have to go and get some petrol, the can is empty.'

He peered in, saw Jenny sitting at the table and flashed his killer smile. 'Hi Jenny, glad you're looking after Zelda; these town girls need us country folk to help them survive.'

'What cheek,' Zelda laughed, 'I could teach you a thing or two.' Then frowned realising it was best not to encourage him.

'OK that's fine about the petrol Cador,' she added, her manner cool and dismissive, then shut the door.

'Where were we Jenny? Obviously, Tommy thought a lot of you as he painted your portrait and you socialised together. Were you an item?'

Jenny shook her head. 'No the age difference was too great. Tommy always said if he had been twenty years younger it would have been a different story, but we got on well and he was great company.'

Zelda studied Jenny carefully. She was very pretty; no wonder Tommy was interested.

'Have you always lived here?' she asked.

'I was born in St Ives where my parents still live. My father owns a small art gallery, and my mother has one of the many Cornish pasty shops. I must take you to meet them one day, you will like them.'

Zelda smiled. 'I would like that very much', she said. 'My mother died when I was just two years old and I was brought up by my Grandmother and her second husband. They were lovely, and we lived in a big house in Hampstead. You're so lucky to have two parents living. Have you ever strayed outside Cornwall?'

Jenny patted Prince who had come into the kitchen in the hope of a biscuit. 'I had several years working on cruise ships as a nurse, it was quite fun to see other countries, or at least their ports, but after a while I missed Cornwall; however, I'd saved enough money by then to buy my house.'

'Well done you.' Zelda said', Can you tell me what finally happened to Tommy?'

Jenny took a deep breath. 'Well, a couple were walking along the top of the cliff overlooking Smugglers Cove; it can only be reached at low tide.'

Zelda nodded, 'The dogs and I went there yesterday.' she said. 'These people looked over the edge and saw a body lying on the beach'. Jenny continued, 'They rang Emergency and as it was high tide, a helicopter was sent and landed in the Cove. They found it was Tommy, who had apparently been sketching some sea birds sitting on their nests. They reckon he was halfway up the cliff when he fell. His sketchbook was beside him, and his neck was broken. There was an inquest. The Coroner returned an open verdict, as no one could be sure whether Tommy slipped or perhaps had a dizzy spell, causing him to fall down the cliff to the beach below. The whole village turned out for the funeral and we gave him a good send off at the Anchor afterwards.'

'What a sad end to an exciting life,' Zelda said, 'I do so wish I had met him. I'm still no nearer unravelling the mystery of why he left me everything. The money was not a lot but with my own savings, I have enough to make this place as I want it. Then I can live here for perhaps six months before I need to start earning again. I'm hoping that when I tackle clearing the studio, I may find something that may throw a bit of light on how Tommy and I are connected, at the moment it doesn't make any sense.'

A thought suddenly struck her, and Zelda quickly got up from the table. 'Excuse me a minute, I have something for you.'

With that, she ran upstairs, and quickly returned with the picture of Jenny that she had found the other night. 'There you are, now you have a pair.' she said a trifle breathlessly.

Jenny took the picture and looked at it with misty eyes. 'That's so kind of you, I'll now have one each side of the fireplace. I'll try to remember if Tommy ever said anything that will help you solve all this. 'Now I must get going, I have promised to meet my sister, Patti for lunch.'

They walked to the front door and as she was about to leave, Jenny said, 'By the way I meant to tell you about Mad Iris. She's a mysterious figure you may see around, she lives in that big house on the hill above here called Hawke Hall, the one with the two turrets. No one has ever known Mad Iris buy food and the local children say she eats babies. Of course, it's nonsense but she is weird.'

Zelda laughed. 'What an interesting place this is, whatever next?'

'Who knows but I hope it's nice. Thanks for the coffee Zelda'. Jenny said kissing her on the cheek, and clutching her picture as she walked off down the path.

# CHAPTER 5
# GRACE

Upstairs, Zelda wandered into her bedroom deep in thought, mulling over what Jenny had told her about Tommy. However, she was no nearer finding out why she had come into her inheritance. Once again, she sat on the end of her bed and looked at the silver framed photos on the chest of drawers. If only you were here Grandma Grace perhaps, you could tell me she thought.

The photo of a laughing young girl, with very short curly hair stared back at her. The photo had originally been in a frame outside a large department store in Oxford Street. This was at a time when up to the minute girls were cutting their hair short, and Grace had been one of the first in London to adopt the new style. The chief stylist of the hairdressing salon in the store said he would cut and style her hair for free, if they could take a photo of her and display it in a glass-fronted case outside. Therefore, for months Grace had smiled out at buses, taxis and hurrying shoppers in busy Oxford Street.

Zelda had loved the tales Grace used to tell her of her modelling days. How she had swept down the runways at the famous designers' seasonal shows, in dresses with tight skirts and matching little hats, covered in cabochon decorations. Sometimes Grace opened the show in a stunning day dress and sometimes she was the bride that closed the show, but always to wild applause. That was when the stick thin models would arrive with their little cases containing, their makeup, massive false eyelashes, waspies to make their waists smaller and falsies to pad out their busts if needed.

Zelda liked the tale of how Grace and several other models had strutted around an empty shop window of a big department store in Oxford Circus, which had drawn massive crowds, not to mention dirty old men in raincoats pressed up against the glass. Eventually the police stopped these new concept shows, citing the huge crowds thronging the pavement as a hazard. Grace had also been part of teatime fashion shows in the restaurant of one of the poshest stores in London. Parading between the customers' tables, sometimes slipping off a fur coat and dragging it along behind her.

Another time, she said, an ex-boyfriend had been sitting enjoying his tea with a new girlfriend, when Grace passing by, had done a twirl and given him a wink, much to his embarrassment. Both Grace and Zelda laughed at this tale.

Grace had married Eddie; the boyfriend she had known since her teen years. Theirs had been an on off romance. They had both dated other people after their many falling outs, but after a while, always got back together again.

'I was an idiot,' Grace had told Zelda, 'the writing was on the wall, we just didn't get on. In those days you didn't live together before you married, it was just not done. Therefore, you didn't really know what each other was like. It came as a nasty shock when the boy you had gone to the cinema and dances with turned out to be nothing like the one you woke up with when you were married. The only plus point was that we had Margarita.'

'That was my mother wasn't it?' Zelda would ask.

'Yes, darling,' Grace would reply with tears in her eyes. 'Margarita was the most perfect baby you ever saw. Eddie was unable to support us, so I continued modelling and being the breadwinner. Several years later at a party, I met Jonny, a very successful and divorced stockbroker. It was just one of those things. To think that we should not be together was impossible. Therefore, Eddie and I divorced and Jonny and I married at Caxton Hall, and we lived in Hampstead. Margarita, after leaving school, enrolled at the leading stage and dance academy where she shone. It was not long before she was asked to take the lead in a West End show. After that, it was films, first small parts then second leads. The down side was she did get a bit wild. Margarita got pregnant, something that could ruin a career in those days. She would not talk about it and after you were born, she named you Zelda after a character in a book she had been reading. At the time, she was living in a rambling house in Notting Hill with another actress and a fashion model. Whoever was not working looked after you. It was all rather bohemian but it worked. Then while making a film she met Jacques, the French leading man and they became engaged. They arranged to meet in Paris. Margarita drove there in her little sports car and while negotiating the big roundabout in the centre of Paris she was involved in a horrendous accident...' The story usually stopped there, as Grace could not go on.

Once Zelda asked, 'Was that why you and Jonny looked after me?'

Grace then smiled and said, 'Yes darling, that was the only good outcome of the tragic and sad event.'

Still curious Zelda asked what had happened to Eddie, after all he was her real grandfather.

'He opened a bar near Benidorm in Spain,' Grace would reply, 'it did very well, but I think Eddie drank most of the profits and I never heard of him again. That was a long time ago.'

Zelda had a picture in her mind of this rather louche character standing outside his bar. Beside him was a sign on a board that read 'BRITISH ALL DAY BREAKFAST.' The weather would be glorious and a drink would always be in Eddie's hand as he cracked jokes with anyone passing by.

'Why did you call my mother Margarita?' Zelda had asked.

Grace smiled, and said, 'when I was at school Rita Hayworth had been a famous film star. I went to the cinema two or three times a week with my friends and she was the person we all wanted to look like. Films at that time were pure escapism; nothing bad went unpunished and most ended happily. The film 'Gilda' was our favourite at the time, and Rita Hayworth who was at her sexiest and glamourous best, starred in it. Therefore, when it came to the time to name our baby, I insisted she would be Margarita, which was Rita Hayworth's real name.'

Zelda, hearing the dogs getting restless downstairs, stood up and sighed. Well at least I come from an interesting family, she thought, just a shame I didn't know most of them.

# CHAPTER 6
# MAD IRIS

The next day when Zelda took the dogs for their morning walk, a thick mist rolled in off the sea. Rounding the corner to Smugglers Cove an odd sight came into view. Standing on the furthest rock, which was partially covered by the waves, stood an old woman with wild tangled, red hair. She was wearing a long shapeless gown and standing with her arms outstretched staring out to sea.

Suddenly she began singing scales in a harsh, high voice. Over and over again. Up and down, up and down. It was too much for the dogs who sat down, and pointing their noses upwards, started to howl.

Zelda looked anxiously at the figure on the rocks but the old woman didn't turn around. For reasons she could not explain, Zelda felt very afraid, thinking this was hardly the behaviour of a sane person. Eventually the dogs stopped howling and followed her over the rocks back to the bay, where she began to enjoy its calmness and quiet. Then the sun finally broke through and started to burn the mist away.

Cador was in the garden when Zelda returned to the house after a much longer walk than normal just to calm her nerves.

'Gosh I am pleased you are here,' she said. Then recounted the scene she had witnessed at Smugglers Cove.

Cador laughed, 'That was Mad Iris; she believes she is the reincarnation of Madame Melba, the legendary opera singer, and never stops practising her scales. If you ever go near her house, you can hear her singing them for hours on end.'

Zelda shook her head, 'Not me,' she said, 'I'll stay as far away from her as possible, she gives me the creeps. How does she get to the cove? I didn't see her going down to the beach in front of us.'

'That is a mystery. No one has ever seen how Mad Iris gets there, people say she just suddenly materialises. Locals reckon that she is, as she claims, indeed the reincarnation of Madame Melba, and being a spirit, only appears when it suits her. She lives alone in that big old house and never uses lights, only candles. What with all that and never being seen buying food she is a bit more than just eccentric.'

Zelda smiled up at Cador, he really was quite sweet. She looked round the garden with amazement. No wonder he had removed his shirt. The grass had been cut, the edges trimmed. Both ponds had been cleared of the choking pondweed and the rushes were now an acceptable amount, leaving the pond lilies to float happily between the stepping-stones. The flowerbeds were devoid of weeds, dead flowers removed and any eatable fruit sat in wicker baskets beneath the trimmed apple and plum trees.

'Oh Cador you have done a wonderful job, I had no idea this was such a beautiful place.'

Cador looked pleased and shrugged his broad shoulders. 'All in the day's work. Now you can see that you have a barbeque area over there, and up at the end of the garden is a wooden sided compost heap. You can put any dead flowers and your grass cuttings in there out of sight. In the small pond that was nearly hidden from view by the tropical plants, tall grasses and Eastern statues you have newts and frogs. The big pond has lots of Koi and Goldfish. When no one was living here I used to come up and feed them, I didn't like to think of them dying.'

Zelda felt bad that she had not been nicer to him. 'That was so kind of you, when I have my house warming barbeque you must come' she said.

Cador nodded. 'Now let me show you how to use the mower, just sit on it and put your hands on the controls.'

Zelda did as instructed, Cador stood behind, leant forward and covered her hands with his. She could feel his warmth through her thin Tee shirt. Immediately she jumped up and gave him an imperious look.

'We had one of these mowers at my previous house so I know how to use it thank you.' Her voice was chilling.

Cador smiled, 'Well it was worth a try,' he said grinning broadly.

'You are shameless,' she rebuked him. Then thawed a bit as she realised it was just his way with the opposite sex.

Putting on a broad Cornish accent, Cador said. 'Sorry ma'am, we rough local boys know no better.'

In spite of herself Zelda laughed, 'Just send me your account and thanks, the garden looks lovely.'

# CHAPTER 7
# TOMMY'S ROOM

With the garden under control, Zelda reluctantly turned her attention to Tommy's studio. As she was sadly lacking in artistic talent there was no reason to keep it as a studio, it would make a superb guest annexe. Feeling that to poke around in someone's private world was intrusive, even if they were no longer around, she had put this off as long as possible but it had to be done.

First, she sorted through the piles of canvases putting aside half a dozen that really appealed to her, with the intention of having them dotted round the house once they were in frames. They ranged from paintings of houses on stilts, that she felt Tommy had done while living in Bolinas, to one of tousled haired young men playing musical instruments. Was this a portrait of the rock group that Tommy had formed with his fellow students?

Another was of a young girl with dreamy eyes. As Zelda studied the beautiful face, she felt sad, but didn't know why. The eyes, the hair, the oval shaped face were perfect. I will have this framed and it will hang in the hall for all to see, Zelda thought. It will be one of my favourite possessions.

Next, after gathering all the artist's materials, paints, brushes, pencils and various items into a cardboard box that she found under the bench, Zelda ran downstairs and put them in the boot of her car with the remaining canvases and the wooden easel. After checking through the papers and magazines, she kept the magazine containing the photo of her and Donald but binned the rest. It took most of the afternoon to clean the studio. The splashes of paint were impossible to remove so Zelda decided it made sense to have carpet fitted, and tile the shower room and kitchenette area sometime soon.

Another task she had put on the back burner was Tommy's bedroom. A bedroom was such a personal thing, but it couldn't remain as it was, so grabbing a load of black sacks she set to work.

To start with, Zelda emptied the drawers of clothes, only saving the tee shirts that had logos of American cities and images of rock stars. Some of the rock stars were well known and some she didn't recognise at all. However, this could be memorabilia that fans would love to possess. The personal items such as documents, watches, rings and his wallet, she put in one of the two smaller top drawers, to be dealt with later. In the wardrobe, as well as loafers and trainers there were only jeans and jackets. Tommy had obviously been a casual dresser and not a suit wearer. Everything went into the growing pile of black sacks apart from the tee shirts and the two bomber jackets with big splashy designs on the back. Looking round, the room was tidy but it needed something to say Tommy had been here, and then remembering the two guitars Zelda ran and fetched them. Propped up against the wall she viewed the result, head on one side, and now the bedroom passed muster. Nearly but not quite impersonal, there was only a hint of its previous occupant.

It was now evening and after feeding the dogs Zelda realised how hungry she was. Too late to cook, I'll go to the Anchor, and with that she took the MG and drove along the coast road, admiring the sunset as it turned the sky a brilliant, fiery red.

# CHAPTER 8
# HARRISON

When Zelda walked up to the bar to order a much-needed glass of wine she noted how busy it was. 'Hello, can I have a glass of house red please?' She said to the bar tender who looked a trifle young to be pulling pints.

As she turned round to look for a vacant table, a familiar face smiled at her in recognition.

'Well if it isn't Queen Anne, how nice to bump into you again.'

Zelda looked up at the smiling face and remembered her first walk on the beach with the dogs. 'Harrison of course. Are you still here completing your TV program?'

Harrison nodded and said, 'This is my last day working here for a couple of weeks, it's back to London in the morning to finalise the editing. Would you let me buy you dinner, I hate eating alone?'

Zelda paid the barman and took a sip of her wine while she weighed up the situation. Did a chance meeting on a beach make it reasonable to accept sharing a meal with an almost total stranger? It would certainly be nicer than dining alone.

'Thanks, I would like that, and you can tell me all about your exciting job. I think that table over there has just become vacant, shall we grab it?'

Harrison led the way to the table by the window and held her chair out until she had taken her seat. Hmm, good manners, Zelda thought.

It turned out to be a jolly meal. They both had steak and chips. Zelda thinking of the drive back refused the offer of a top up although she would have enjoyed it while Harrison had a large red wine. Jenny and a tall, blond man, who she introduced as Alvar, a friend from Sweden, passed their table and stopped for a chat. Alvar it seemed had been working on the cruise ships at the same time as Jenny and they had kept in touch.

'Jenny you are just the person I hoped to see. I want to go to St Ives to a charity shop with some of Tommy's things. Will you come with me?'

Jenny thought for a moment, 'I was going at the weekend so that will work out well.'

Zelda gave her a big smile, 'You're a star', she said, 'I'll be outside your house about ten thirty, if that's OK and we can make a day of it.'

Seeing Jenny give Harrison a quizzical look Zelda said, 'This is Harrison a new friend of mine, we met on the beach and he is making a documentary about this area, isn't that exciting?'

Jenny laughed. 'Wonderful can't wait. Nice to meet you Harrison, and now we will leave you both to finish your meal.'

When they were once again alone Harrison asked who Tommy was?

Zelda sighed saying, 'I wish I knew it's the oddest thing. A recent last will and testament discovered in the house I now live in proved to be genuine. I inherited everything, the house, all Tommy's possessions and any money in his bank accounts. I was absolutely dumbfounded, but I was at a stage in my life when a new beginning was just what I needed, so here I am.'

Harrison let out a low whistle. 'That is an amazing story. Tommy obviously knew who you were, but what was the connection. Are there any clues that you can pursue?'

Zelda shook her head. 'I'm sure I will find out eventually, although Tommy was English, he had lived in America from his early twenties up to three years ago when he came to Cornwall. Jenny was friends with Tommy, in fact, he painted her portrait, but she has no idea how I fit into all this. Now tell me about your life, which part of the country are you from?'

Harrison smiled; it was a proper smile that started in his very blue eyes before reaching his mouth, which parted to show perfect white teeth.

'Mother was very home counties, my father came from Ireland and we lived in Surrey, so a bit of a mixture really. Currently I'm living in a bachelor flat in London following a rather bitter split from my wife. We didn't have children, which I suppose is lucky, it was just that my job took me away a lot and Giselle got bored.'

Zelda thought what a nice voice he had, warm and with a slight drawl that could come from his Irish connection.

'Did you go to Ireland much?' she asked.

'I spent a lot of holidays with my grandmother in Dublin, I know I picked up a twang,' he said laughing.

'No it's nice,' Zelda said and changed the subject quickly not wanting to sound sycophantic, 'I'm having a small house warming barbeque the weekend after next would you like to come?'

Harrison looked pleased. 'Yes, I'll make sure I'm back again by then so that would be nice. Where exactly do you live?'

Zelda looked at her watch and could not believe how the time had flown. 'Marryat House, it's just above the beach where you saw me with the dogs. Talking of dogs, I had better get back or they will think I have run off.'

As Zelda got up to go, Harrison said, 'I'll walk you to your car. I'm staying here at the Anchor tonight'.

When they reached the MGB, Zelda turned and faced Harrison. 'Thank you for the meal that was most enjoyable. About seven for the barbeque then,' and held out her hand.

Harrison ignored it and suddenly bent forward and kissed her unexpectedly on the mouth. Surprised she didn't move. It was nice; in fact, it was very nice. After a while, Zelda stepped back, glad it was quite dark and hoping no one had seen that kiss, she knew what small communities were like. Trying to keep her voice normal, although she felt unexpectedly flustered, Zelda quickly got into the car and said firmly, 'Thanks again Harrison, bye.'

With that, she started the engine and sped away aware that Harrison was still standing and staring after her retreating car.

# CHAPTER 9
# TIDYING UP

The days flew by in a flurry of work. Big men in overalls were all over the house. The glazier replaced the broken panes of glass in the conservatory. A firm of painters and decorators recommended by Cador, stripped out the bench in the studio, sanded the floor and then painted the whole annexe a lovely pale yellow. Zelda took refuge in the garden, only popping in occasionally to make numerous cups of tea to keep them all going, then retreated back to the garden to keep out of their way.

By now, the grass had grown quite long and needed cutting. After wrestling with the mower for a few minutes, it fired into life and Zelda sat astride the big beast enjoying seeing the neat lines return to the cropped lawns.

As she sat on the mower going up and down the garden, Zelda noticed things that needed tackling. A rockery round the bottom of an apple tree was overgrown, the statues and birdbaths in the tropical plant area needed cleaning and likewise the barbeque area. Finding a wire brush in the shed Zelda set about cleaning the barbeque. Moss had grown between the cracks in the bricks and a host of creepy crawlies had made their homes under the metal tray designed to hold the charcoal. I must check how much charcoal is in the shed, she thought, stopping to stand back and admire her work. Then glancing up towards the hill above the garden realised that she had a perfect view of Hawke Hall where Mad Iris lived. The windows in the two turrets set each side of the roof stared out over the land to the sea beyond. What a wonderful place to spy from, perhaps wreckers had lived there long ago, signalling to boats that then smashed against the rocks. Stop dreaming, she thought, not all Cornwall had been populated with these romantic characters.

It was the middle of the afternoon before Zelda finally finished in the garden and the dogs were getting restless. Calling them to heel, she crossed the road and headed for Smugglers Cove.

At the beach, the dogs ran ahead, chasing each other up and down by the water's edge. Zelda stood and watched them thinking how happy they were, when they suddenly stopped and stood quivering. Puzzled, she turned round and let out a gasp as she came face to face with a wizened old woman she recognised as Mad Iris. How had this frightening apparition appeared? There had been no one on the beach when she and the dogs arrived and surely, she would have noticed anyone coming over the rocks to get to this spot.

'Don't know you?' The voice was raspy, and when she spoke, the thin lips parted to show broken and stained teeth, 'I am Madame Melba and I am very famous.'

Zelda fought her desire to run away; instead she forced a smile and said, 'Yes I've heard of you Madame Melba. The dogs and I were just leaving.'

The old woman put a claw like hand on her arm. 'No stay and hear me sing dear.'

Zelda called the dogs. Reluctantly they came to her side, tails down and shivering. 'Sorry we have to go,' she said and strode away as fast as she could.

The sound of Mad Iris practising her scales floated after her on the warm afternoon air. Back at the house, Zelda made a strong cup of tea to calm her nerves and tried to figure out how Mad Iris had managed to materialise out of nowhere, and appear beside her on the beach.

# CHAPTER 10
# ST IVES

Saturday morning dawned bright and clear. After picking Jenny up at her house, Zelda drove to St Ives, both of them chatting away and enjoying the scenery along the coast road. Jenny wanted to know about Harrison.

'He looked like he was quite smitten with you,' she said.

'Nonsense,' Zelda laughed, 'we hardly know each other. I think he looks at all the girls like that. That is one expert romancer but he is very attractive, besides I'm not looking for any attachments, all I want is a quiet life and to solve the mystery of Tommy.'

Arriving in St Ives, Jenny gave the directions to a charity shop where they unloaded the black sacks and carried them inside. Next, up a side road they parked the car behind the art gallery owned by Jenny's father. When they entered through the front door, Zelda noted that the main gallery caught the light from three skylights set high up in the roof. On the white walls hung a variety of framed pictures, some depicting local scenes, some still life paintings and the remainder colourful abstract studies.

Jenny introduced her father as Miles. Shaking his hand Zelda liked him immediately. Not wasting time as there were several customers browsing round the gallery, Zelda gave him a winning smile and said. 'I have some pictures outside that I found in the studio when I moved into my house. Can I get you to have a look at them and give me your opinion please? I mean are they any good or not?'

Miles returned her smile saying, 'Of course, bring them into the back office and I will give them the once over. '

It took a couple of trips to bring the pictures from the car and then Miles called his assistant to take over and joined Jenny and Zelda.

'Who did you say the artist was'? Miles queried as he lifted each one carefully on to a table.

Zelda took a deep breath, 'The ones signed TT we know were painted by Tommy Tree, but the two abstracts I have no idea about.'

Miles looked up, a surprised expression on his face. 'Not Tommy Tree, lead singer and guitarist of the 'Tommy and the T Men' group? I used to buy their records years ago.'

The girls looked at him amazed that he had heard of Tommy.

'Yes that's the person who left me the house and all his possessions. He even painted a couple of pictures of Jenny,' Zelda said, 'But I didn't know he was so famous.'

Miles was looking at a painting of the four young men playing on a stage. His eyes had a faraway look as he said, 'Well it was quite a while ago but believe me if these pictures were auctioned and fans of Tommy knew, they would fetch quite a lot of money. In addition, the two abstract paintings are by a very collectible artist and fetch big prices on the world art market. I think Tommy has left you a small fortune here, I cannot believe it.'

Zelda thought for a bit then said, 'Miles can I ask you to handle the selling of them for me on a purely business basis, with you getting a percentage of the selling price? Also, as you were a fan of Tommy's music, please choose one picture for yourself. I have kept several back that I really like, and I will display them round the house once they are in frames.'

Miles held out his hand. 'Deal,' he said, 'Thank you so much, I'll get the best prices I can for them. Now while you are here we'll list them and you'll have a copy, so it is all on a business like footing.'

It took a good hour to describe and enter all the paintings on the computer and print a list for Zelda to take away. As she was about to leave, Zelda remembered the box of Tommy's art materials in the car and ran outside returning with the heavy box.

'Do you know of a struggling young artist who would make good use of these, they belonged to Tommy.'

Miles thought for while then said, 'Not a young artist but I know of an old retired fisherman who has taken up art and has a wonderful raw talent, he would love these. Thank you Zelda, you really are a lovely, kind person.'

Mission accomplished, Zelda and Jenny said goodbye, and wandered off down the cobbled streets looking at the various shops selling tourist gifts and locally made clothes.

When they arrived at the high street Jenny stopped at one of the shops selling Cornish Pasties.

'This is owned by my mother,' she said and taking Zelda's arm propelled her into the shop.

'Hey Mum, come and meet Zelda,' she called out, and a very attractive woman, who was an older version of Jenny stepped out from behind the counter.

'So this is Zelda,' she said, 'Jenny has told me all about you. I'm Karen and you are just as Jenny described.'

Zelda smiled looking round the busy shop. 'What a huge selection of pasties, I can't believe you do such a variety of fillings.'

Karen put a couple of pasties in a bag. 'There you are, our two best sellers for you to try.' and handed the bag to Zelda.

'Oh thank you, I'll enjoy them,' she said and opened her handbag to pay.

Karen shook her head, 'They are a small present; I hear you have taken over Tommy's place. How are you getting on?'

'OK thanks. I'm having a small barbeque next Saturday as a house warming, would you and Miles like to come? Jenny's coming so do please try, it starts about seven o'clock but if you're late it won't matter. You have a bit of a drive to get to my place. '

Glancing round at the queue of people waiting to buy their pasties, Zelda quickly said goodbye then she and Jenny left the shop and made their way to the harbour.

Jenny knew most of the restaurants that lined the harbour and recommended one that specialised in fish. Zelda ordered Lobster Thermidor, her all-time favourite and Jenny, who was watching her weight, chose Lemon Sole.

While they waited for their order to arrive, Jenny said, 'You are inviting quite a few people to your barbeque, where are you planning to buy the burgers and chicken?'

Zelda had no idea, so she said. 'I was hoping you would help me with that.'

Jenny thought for a minute, 'There's a Farmers' Market on Fridays and Saturdays in the town, I would go there first, they do really fresh produce.'

Then the waiter arrived with their order. 'Ah, here's our food.' Zelda said, thinking how am I going to find room for half a large lobster, covered in a creamy sauce topped with parmesan cheese and breadcrumbs, grilled so the top is crunchy. Not to mention it's on a bed of lettuce and accompanied with French bread.

'Good advice. I'll try the Market first, that's if I don't die of over eating,' she said, picking up her knife and fork, 'shall we start, this looks fabulous?'

It proved to be as wonderful as it looked and Zelda smiled happily at Jenny. 'I'm so glad I landed up here in Cornwall. Life has taken a definite turn for the better.'

# CHAPTER 11
# RICK

It was the day before the barbeque and as luck would have it, the weather forecast was for a fine weekend. Zelda had just returned from the Farmers' Market and was putting all the food into the American style refrigerator. As the shelves filled up, she reflected how lucky it was that Tommy had bought a large fridge freezer. Job done, she was just going to make a cup of coffee when there was a knock on the door.

The dogs got there first and stood, noses pressed against the door, waiting to see who was outside. When Zelda opened the door, she saw a pleasant looking man standing with a hesitant expression on his face.

'I'm trying to locate someone called Zelda,' he said in a slightly American accent.

'Well you have come to the right place. I'm Zelda, how can I help?'

Zelda immediately felt that this was going to be very revealing but how she had no idea. The man reached into his pocket and produced a long white envelope.

'This is for you, can I come in?' he said.

Zelda stepped back saying, 'Of course please follow me.' And led the way into the kitchen.

On the way the man said, 'My name is Rick, I'm staying at the Anchor pub, just down the road.'

Zelda smiled, 'yes, everyone stays there; it's the hub of the village.'

When they were both seated at the kitchen table Rick handed over the envelope which had 'Zelda' and the house address written on the front in a strong scrawl.

'This was given to me by Tommy and I was asked to give it to you if anything happened to him.'

Zelda took the envelope with shaking hands thinking, am I at last going to get answers to the mystery of Tommy? Before opening the letter and giving herself time to regain her composure, Zelda asked Rick how he knew Tommy.

'I was in Tommy's rock group when we were all at art college. We were just four young guys having fun and playing at local hops. I suppose we must have been quite good, as an agent approached us and offered to manage us professionally. When we first signed the contract and went to America, we had no idea that we would make it big. However, as things turned out it was the time when 'Rock and Roll' took off and for years we played to packed houses all over the States. They were wild times as you can guess but we survived.'

Zelda looked at Rick and could just about imagine him as a teenage musician full of the brash chat that went with being up on a stage with girls cheering hysterically.

'What instrument did you play?' She asked, curious to get some idea of how it had been, so long ago.

Rick smiled as he dredged up the scene from the back of his subconscious. 'I was the drummer and harmonised with Tommy, who was our lead guitarist and chief vocalist.'

Leaning forward like a child listening to a bedtime story, Zelda said, 'Please do go on, I'm fascinated.'

Rick returned her smile and resumed. 'Well, when after what was a long time of touring round every State in America, we finally went out of fashion, tensions sprang up and the group disbanded. Tommy rented a house in Bolinas, in Marin County, California and I married and settled down in Muir Valley not far away. The two of us kept in touch and met up at least once a year at the Fireman's Picnic event in Muir Valley. It's organised to raise funds for the volunteer fire department and we would join in and play with the local musicians. It was like we were teenagers again.'

Rick smiled at the recollection and Zelda could imagine the happy scene.

'Tommy decided to return to England where his roots were and bought this house. He chose Cornwall as he had happy memories of childhood holidays spent round these parts. When I last met him in a bar in Bolinas, Tommy was in a very thoughtful mood. 'Now I'm older I have regrets', he told me. 'I didn't behave well to certain people. I must right a terrible wrong.' He then gave me this letter and said that if anything happened to him to give the letter to you.'

Rick leaned back and stared at the unopened letter in Zelda's hand. 'I have no idea what Tommy wrote.' He said.

Carefully Zelda slit open the envelope and removed a single sheet of paper. Unfolding it, she read slowly taking in every word. Rick looked at Zelda and thought how pretty she was, admiring the tumbling, curly chestnut red hair, big tawny coloured eyes and soft pink mouth. When Zelda came to the end of the letter, her expression was one of sadness and relief.

'Thank you so much for bringing me this all the way from America. Tommy explains that he met Margarita, my mother, when he was a student and she was studying at a stage school. They fell madly in love and had a great time together. London was the centre of all that was trendy and happening in the theatre, fashion, films and music world at that time. When Margarita was offered parts in films and became an up and coming film actress predicted for major roles, she found out she was pregnant. Tommy was just about to fly out with his agent and rock group for your first concert tour of America. A bitter row ensued. Tommy told Margarita to get an abortion and they parted on bad terms. Margarita didn't have the abortion and after I was born, she wrote to Tommy and told him he was the father of a girl called Zelda. Tommy explains he was enjoying his life as a rock star and didn't reply. At the end of the letter, he asks me to forgive him and hopes that leaving me everything will go some way to make amends.'

Rick was amazed at the revelations in the letter. Like all rock stars, Tommy had been romantically linked to many girls but he had never mentioned Margarita, and Rick had never seen her at any of their gigs before they left for the States.

'Are you OK Zelda?' he said, 'this must have been quite a shock to you'

Zelda, who had gone quite pale, got up from her chair.

'I think I need a drink of some sort', she said, 'I can offer you a glass of whisky or sherry, will you join me?'

Rick nodded, 'too right,' he said, 'a Scotch on the rocks would be great; there're still some questions I want to ask you.'

Zelda found two glasses, filling one with cubes of ice and a measure of Scotch whisky and the other with a large amount of sherry.

'Let's go into the conservatory, I can see this turning into quite a long chat, that's if you don't have any plans'

Rick shook his head, 'no I really came to see you. I have relations in London that I will visit before I catch the plane back to California, but there's no hurry.'

When they were seated in the conservatory, drinks in hand, Zelda leaned back in her chair and sipped her sherry. It had a relaxing effect, and a sudden thought crossed her mind.

'Can you come to a small party I'm having tomorrow? It's a barbecue and quite informal. I'll be able to introduce you to the father of a friend of mine, who was a big fan of Tommy and the T Men.'

Rick swirled the ice round in his glass and smiled. 'Fancy that, nice to know we're still remembered over here. Yes, I would love to come, thank you.'

They chatted on, Rick telling Zelda more about his and Tommy's lives as rock stars.

'I still cannot believe, after all this time, that my father was a famous person. I come from two famous showbiz people but I never had any talent in that direction. What was he like Rick, as a person I mean?' She asked.

Rick thought for a while before saying. 'You would have liked him Zelda. He had great charm and girls made a beeline for him, even before he was famous. I feel very sorry he didn't marry your mother but I can see a huge likeness between you and Tommy. The same mannerisms and even the way you tilt your head to one side when you talk, and of course the red hair.'

Zelda was pleased, she had never realised before that not knowing either of her parents had meant so much to her, however, now she felt nearer to them.

Rick got up from his chair. 'Thanks for the drink and invitation. I'll be here for your party tomorrow; what time shall I arrive?' he said kissing Zelda on the cheek.

'About seven,' she replied, 'thank you Rick for coming all this way to see me. I feel less of an orphan now, strange that.'

As she watched Rick drive away, she wondered what other surprises were in store for her.

# CHAPTER 12
# THE BARBEQUE

The day of the barbeque dawned bright and warm. Zelda had been to the Farmers' Market and returned with beef burgers, sausages and chicken quarters from the butcher there, who had recommended another stand for rolls and readymade salads of the exotic type.

'Why get hot and flustered when I can appear cool as a cucumber,' she joked with the girl at the stand.'

Then she drove home thrilled with her purchases. Any way, if I put the salads in my own dishes, who will know I have not slaved away, chopping all morning.

Arriving back at the house she found Cador already parked there.

'Hi, she said, 'what are you up to Caldor?'

'Nothing yet,' he twinkled, 'but I live in hope. Actually, I have come to offer my help. When Tommy had parties here I used to put up lights in the garden and sort out the barbeque for him. If you like, as I know where things are I can do the same for you today.'

A weight lifted off Zelda's shoulders and she beamed at Cador. 'Thank you so much, that would be lovely, as it's the first entertaining I've done here, I was a bit apprehensive. If you do that I will sort out the glasses and plates and things.'

Cador nodded and went off whistling. How lovely to have a capable man about the place Zelda thought, staring at his tall figure striding purposefully up the garden.

Soon all the food was ready and placed with the wine to keep cool in the refrigerator. Not for the first time did Zelda bless Tommy for buying a big double doored model with the icemaker on the front. Looking out of the kitchen window, she could see Cador had strung lights in the trees and moved several of the picnic benches and seats to round the barbeque area. Quickly she made some beef sandwiches and took them with a couple of cans of beer out into the garden.

'Wow, beef with mustard sandwiches, my absolute favourite.' Cador said. He sat eating happily and then opened the cans of beer, a faraway look in his eyes. Suddenly he leant forward and fixed her with his dark, smouldering gaze and said huskily, 'Darling Zelda, I think you are really lovely and it so happens I don't have a girlfriend at the moment, would you be my girlfriend? I know it's rather cheeky of me to ask but.'…. His voice trailed off thinking Zelda might be a bit out of his league.

The question hung in the air until Zelda said quietly. 'Thank you Cador but I'm really happy here at the moment and I'm not looking for any new romantic entanglements.'

Cador smiled ruefully and drained his beer saying, 'Just a mad idea but I won't give up.'

To change the subject Zelda said quickly. 'Oh by the way a big mystery has been cleared up. Yesterday I had a visit from Rick, an old friend of Tommy's from their 'Rock and Roll' days. He's coming tonight so you'll meet him. Rick gave me a letter that Tommy had written some time ago. It was to be given to me if anything happened to him. It turns out that Tommy was my father.'

Cador whistled, 'That explains why you got the house, what a shame you two never met.'

Zelda nodded and said, 'But at least I now know who my father was and that ends a mystery that has dogged me all my life. My grandmother always somehow avoided my questions and after a while I never asked.'

The dogs bounded up, barking and putting their wet noses on Zelda's bare arms. 'I think they want their afternoon run,' she said patting their sleek heads.

Cador stood up and kissed her lightly on the cheek. 'I'll go home now but I'll be back before seven o'clock to light the barbeque.'

'Thanks, see you tonight.' Zelda called after him, and then with the dogs in tow she made her way down to the beach.

Later in her bedroom, Zelda surveyed the contents of her wardrobe. What she wanted was to look casual but also sophisticated. Harrison said he would be there and she felt excited at the thought. As he inhabited the media world, he would be used to girls who were up to the minute and she was not a country bumpkin yet. After discarding several outfits, she chose a pair of yellow, flared crepe trousers and a low cut floral top that she had bought on the trip to St Ives with Jenny. Adding long dangly earrings, several hoop bracelets and high wedge sandals she surveyed herself in the mirror. Satisfied, she then forgot all about how she looked and ran downstairs as the first guest arrived.

By eight o'clock Marryat House was a colourful, noisy scene as guests stood or sat around drinking, laughing and watching Cador expertly turning food on the barbeque. He had arrived with Maisie, the barmaid from the Anchor, who could not believe her luck when Cador had asked her to come with him. Even though it was rather short notice, she had some time owing and the Manager said he would cover for her.

Jenny arrived with her sister Patti, who was curious to meet Zelda, having heard so much about the glamourous new resident. Joe, the garage owner, turned up with his wife and Rick, who had accepted a lift in Joe's car. They had got talking in the bar of the Anchor about cars, as men do.

Jenny's parents, Karen and Miles arrived from St Ives and were most impressed by the house and its position. 'How lovely to be able to look out at the sea and have such a beautiful garden,' Karen said, holding Zelda's hand as she gazed round.

That only left Harrison. Perhaps he had forgotten. As Zelda predicted, Miles and Rick hit it off straight away. Rick telling Miles about the early days when Tommy and the other members had first formed the group.

'Would you like to see the guitars I have upstairs?' Zelda said and led the way up to the annex.

Rick stared at the two rather ancient guitars with a nostalgic look. 'Those were the first guitars Tommy ever played. They're real collectors' items.'

The doorbell rang so Zelda quickly excused herself and ran down the stairs. When she opened the door there stood Harrison clutching a bottle of wine and a bunch of flowers.

'Sorry I'm late, the meeting I was at dragged on and on.' he said, kissing her on both the cheeks.

'On a Saturday! You work far too hard.' she said, taking the wine and flowers while thinking that he was quite the theatrical luvie. 'Thanks for these, come with me into the garden and I'll introduce you to the others.'

It was getting dark and the lights Cador had strung between the trees twinkled prettily, the barbeque glowed and flared as Cador turned over the food he was cooking.

Harrison smiled down at Zelda. 'Magic' he said, 'what a clever girl you are'.

Not me, Zelda thought, this is mostly Cador's doing. A frown went over Harrisons face as he eyed Cador who looked very much in control of things.

'Is that your boyfriend?' he said.

Zelda laughed. 'Good gracious no, we are just good friends.'

'Hmm, he's quite a specimen with his muscles and pony tail.'

'Is he jealous'? Zelda thought but said lightly 'Food or drink first?'

'A drink is what I could do with,' he replied.

They went over to where a table by the kitchen door had a selection of red and white wine, a fruit cup, for those driving and a wide variety of beers. Harrison poured himself a glass of red. 'Here's to us,' he said drinking with a look of satisfaction.

'Us?' Zelda queried.

Before Harrison could answer, the doorbell rang. 'Shall I go?' he asked, 'then you can get on with being hostess.'

Zelda was putting some more baked potatoes out in a dish. Cador was reheating them on the barbeque and had said they were a big success.

'Thanks, I can't think who that can be,' Zelda said, 'I thought everyone was here.'

Harrison disappeared into the hall and Zelda heard the front door open. Then there was an enormous crash and a voice she recognised said, 'That will teach you to mess with my Fiancée.'

Zelda was out of the kitchen and at the front door in a flash. Harrison was out cold on the floor surrounded by broken glass. It was Donald; he was standing outside gazing at his bruised knuckles.

'What are you doing you idiot', she screamed, 'Harrison is only a friend, just opening the door for me as I was busy.'

Donald, his face ghostly in the light from the hall said, 'Well you must have had a reason to run off like that.'

Zelda, her voice shaking with anger replied, 'Yes, I was fed up with you, now go away. I never want to see you again.'

There were running footsteps and Cador launched his toned body at Donald and got him in a judo hold, his arm up his back. 'You heard the lady, now go,' he said, as he marched Donald down to the road and gave him a final push.

Harrison was coming round. 'Was that the wind that blew the door back on me?' he enquired faintly, his chin already bright red.

Zelda and Cador got him to his feet and helped him to the kitchen. Zelda took a bag of frozen peas from the freezer, 'Hold that to your chin to stop the swelling. Now does anything else hurt?'

Harrison shook his head, quite liking the fuss Zelda was making of him. Rick was picking up the broken glass in the hall and Karen, who initially thought the red stains on Harrison's shirt were blood not wine said. 'Give me your shirt before those stains set.'

Like a small boy, he did as he was told. Karen put the shirt in the sink and poured white wine on it before rinsing it out. Zelda, after admiring Harrison's tanned and muscular torso ran upstairs and fetched one of the T-shirts she had found in Tommy's room.

'Here put this on', she said, 'it should fit you.'

By now, the whole party had transferred into the kitchen. Cador was the hero of the hour while Harrison was fussed over by the girls.

'My word,' Jenny said to Zelda. 'How do you do it? All these men fighting over you.'

Zelda was still shaken up. 'I just want a quiet life not this mad merry go round,' she said standing at the sink and rinsing glasses, 'I thought Cornwall would be peaceful, faint hope.'

'Look,' someone shouted, 'up on the hill.' Through the kitchen window, they could see flames leaping from the turreted house, high above them. It was Mad Iris's house.

'Quick Zelda phone the fire brigade.'

Caldor immediately took charge and sped out of the house with Joe in hot pursuit. Seconds later, they heard Joe's car start as the pair of them dashed up the hill to Hawke Hall, which was well alight.

It was only a matter of minutes before the fire engine raced past bells ringing. Everyone stood in the garden looking up. They could hear shouted instructions and see the steam rising as the jets of water touched the seat of the fire.

'I hope Mad Iris managed to get out.' Jenny said, 'she lives all alone with only her cats for company.'

Rick looked puzzled, 'Mad Iris, why is she called that?' he queried.

'Because she thinks she is the now departed opera singer Madame Melba, the one who they named Peach Melba after. You can often hear Mad Iris singing on the beach, but to call it singing is a joke, more like a squawking parrot.' Maisie said. 'When we were kids at school we all used to run and hide if we saw her on the beach. She scared us rigid.'

Joe and Cador returned with the news that the fire was under control but there was no sign of Iris.

'The fire chief reckons that one of her cats knocked a candle over into the huge stack of empty hampers piled up everywhere.' Joe said, rubbing his sooty hand down his face leaving a thick black streak. 'From the labels on them it seems she had a delivery of food every week from an upmarket grocery store in Truro and never got rid of the hampers or boxes. A real rubbish hoarder like a lot of old people.'

'Even though she was odd I hope she is all right'. Jenny said. 'Now that explains why she was never seen shopping locally and why so many rumours started.'

Miles and Karen announced that they were going as they had to get back to St Ives, and after saying their goodbyes, Zelda went with them to the door. As she waved them off a passing car pulled up and a man called out.

'There's someone on the beach down there running round and screaming.' With that, he drove away.

Zelda ran back to the kitchen. 'I think Mad Iris is on the beach. Someone has just said they saw a person there running about screaming.'

Rooting round in a cupboard Zelda found a large torch and called out. 'Come on Cador and Joe, I know the path down to the beach like the back of my hand so I'll lead the way. Jenny darling, you look after Harrison, he's still woozy.'

When they had gone, all the remaining partygoers took themselves into the conservatory, sitting around on the wicker chairs and sofas with their big, comfortable cushions. Jenny and Joanna, Joe's wife, made mugs of coffee and they all tucked into the chocolate brownies and cupcakes that Zelda had left out under plastic, domed covers.

'What a night,' Rick said, 'is it always as hectic as this?'

Joanna munched her brownie. 'Good Lord no,' she exclaimed, 'sometimes we nearly die of boredom. I must say that since Zelda moved here things have livened up somewhat.'

Rick looked at the T-shirt that Harrison was wearing. 'Do you know one of those four guys pictured on the front of that shirt is me? I was the drummer in 'Tommy and the T Men' rock and roll group. We sold those shirts at the concerts we did on our first tour of America. Those were great days and to think Tommy was Zelda's father. I bet he would chuckle if he could see us all here. He was a marvellous guy.'

Harrison squinted down at the logo on his chest. 'Does this make me part of the family?' he said amid laughter.

As Zelda, Cador and Joe arrived at the beach a smoke blackened figure materialised in the beam of the flashlight.

'Big fire up there,' Mad Iris cackled.

'Yes we've seen it.' Cador was the first to speak, puzzled as to how she had managed to get to the beach. 'How did you get here Iris?'

A filthy finger pointed to the cliffs. 'Down the smugglers tunnel from the house, to the cave over there. My name is not Iris, silly boy.'

'Of course, it's Madame Melba,' Cador said.

However, the blackened figure looked at him scornfully and at that moment, the moon came out from behind a cloud. 'Silly boy,' she said, 'I'm Greta Garbo and I want to be alone.'

They then all realised that the shock of the fire had made Iris disorientated and more out of it than before. Joe walked away a few feet and used his mobile phone to call Emergency. Within minutes, an ambulance was on the cliff top and the medics scrambled down.

'Hello,' Zelda said, 'Miss Garbo has had a lucky escape from the house fire, however we think she must have inhaled a lot of smoke and is not very well.'

The medics put a blanket round Iris's shoulders. 'Come along dear,' one said leading her up the beach.

As they walked away, the others could hear Iris's imperious quaver saying.

'How dare you call me dear? I am Greta Garbo the famous film star and I want to be alone.'

When the search party returned, Zelda was pleased to see everyone had found the cakes and were enjoying themselves in the conservatory.

'How did you get on; did you find Mad Iris?' Jenny asked, getting up to make room for Zelda to sit between her and Harrison on one of the sofas.

'No,' Zelda replied, 'we actually found Greta Garbo. Mad Iris has changed her identity and now believes she is the old movie star. It's actually much better, as she no longer sings, which is a relief. The paramedics have taken her to the local hospital and will try and contact her relatives, if they can find any.'

Cador swooped on the brownies. 'Wonderful.' he said, 'do I deserve a coffee as well?'

Joanna got up and looked at Zelda. 'I'll get them, if that's all right with you.'

Zelda gave her a relieved smile. 'Of course, that climb up from the beach was thirsty work.'

Joe said, 'We found out how Mad Iris managed to get to the beach without anyone seeing her. There's a secret tunnel from a cave at the base of the cliffs up to Hawke Hall. Smugglers would use the turret at the Hall to flash lights to boats to tell them when it was safe to come into the bay. The locals would then unload the contraband and take it up to the Hall via the tunnel. I had heard stories from old timers but no one guessed the whereabouts of the tunnel.'

Jenny who was the only one who had ever been to Hawke Hall said. 'I once went there to check she was alright, as she never came to the Surgery. Iris came to the door but wouldn't invite me in. Considering the state of decay and the mess I could see from the door, it's amazing she was never ill.'

After more talk about the evening's events, Rick looked at his watch and remarked that it was time to call it a day. 'Not getting any younger.' he said. 'This will be goodbye Zelda. I'll be off to see my relatives tomorrow but I'll keep in touch.'

At the front door, Zelda hugged him saying, 'Thank you Rick, if you hadn't found me, I would never have known about Tommy.'

Joe and Joanna, who everyone in the village called Mrs Joe, thanked Zelda for a wonderful party and got into their car as they were driving Rick back to the Anchor pub.

Jenny and Patti said it was the best party they had been to for ages and arms linked, they walked a trifle unsteadily, down the road to Jenny's cottage. Cador and Maisie, hand in hand, said it had all been very lovely and exciting and drove off, Maisie glowing with anticipation. Zelda smiled, perhaps Maisie would get what she wanted.

That only left Harrison. 'Are you going to throw me out?' he asked. 'I really don't feel up to driving tonight and you shouldn't be alone in case Thumper returns.'

Zelda laughed, but knew he was pulling the hurt little boy act. However, he was quite right about Donald.

'Thanks, yes Donald could be lurking around. I have a spare bed made up, so you are welcome to stay.' she said, staring into those dazzling blue eyes. 'I'll leave clearing up until the morning; you sit there for a bit and finish your coffee.'

Zelda went to the kitchen door and called the dogs in from the garden. They had been enjoying the odd dropped sausage and discarded roll. 'In your beds,' she ordered making sure, she locked all the outside doors.

'My but you are masterful,' Harrison laughed, 'the coffee is cold, can I have something stronger as a nightcap?'

One drink led to another and they sat side by side chatting idly about the strange happenings of the day. Zelda knew she was feeling relaxed and tipsy, her glass tipped at an alarming angle. Harrison leaned over and took it, placing it on the small table by his side. With an expert manoeuvre, he proceeded to kiss her as she had never been kissed before.

Then Harrison said in that lovely soft voice of his. 'If I'm going to be attacked for something I didn't do, perhaps I should do it. What do you think?'

Zelda dreamily replied, 'Hmm, I think that's fair, considering the circumstances.'

She got up from the sofa and lead the way up the stairs to her bedroom.

# CHAPTER 13
# THE DAY AFTER

It was quite late next morning when Zelda awoke. For a few seconds she couldn't remember how the evening had ended. Then aware of the warm body beside her she blushed as the events of the night flooded back. Harrison stirred as she leant on her elbow and stared at him sleeping. Gosh, he even looked more wonderful asleep. I'm smitten, she thought, that was the last thing I wanted to happen.

Harrison opened his eyes and smiled up at her, 'hallo young lady, who are you?' His tone was low and teasing.

'Someone who is going to let the dogs out into the garden.' Zelda replied, dodging as he made a grab for her. 'I'll be back with a mug of tea in a few minutes.'

Going downstairs and glad of the time to get her thoughts in order, Zelda switched on the kettle. With the dogs in the garden and the tea made, she went upstairs and got back in bed.

Sometime later, there was a knock on the door. Throwing on her dressing gown and running downstairs, Zelda opened the door and there stood a delivery boy with a big bunch of red roses.

'Thank you,' she said taking them and shutting the door.

Harrison came down the stairs to join her. 'Trouble?' he asked.

Zelda looked at the card that was attached to the flowers. 'Oh no,' she exclaimed, 'they're from Donald and he wants to meet me at the hotel he is staying at in Carbis Bay, for a talk. He suggests three o'clock today; do you think I should go?'

Harrison thought for a minute, 'Well, let us have some toast and weigh up the situation.'

Zelda kissed him. How wonderful to have someone to take charge.

Sitting in the kitchen with the toast made, Harrison said. 'I personally think it is best to speak to Donald and tell him exactly what you want to do. If you leave it, he will keep pestering you. However, of course it's up to you. I have to be in St Ives for an early meeting tomorrow morning so I can be near at hand, although I'll not come into the hotel with you.'

Zelda smiled at him. 'That's what I will do then. First, I must clear up in here and in the garden but we have plenty of time for that.'

Harrison put his arms round her, 'Zelda darling, I have wanted you since we first met on the beach. You do like me don't you?'

She sighed heavily, 'Unfortunately yes, I just wanted an uncomplicated life without a man for a while but it seems I have one.' Then she laughed and kissed him. It was getting to be a habit.

With the two of them tidying, Marryat House was eventually back to normal. Showered and glowing Zelda climbed into the MGB and drove off followed by Harrison in his company car.

At St Ives Harrison waved goodbye. His office and studio, with an apartment upstairs were in the town. Zelda continued up the hill and found the newly opened hotel that Donald had mentioned for their talk.

Donald was sitting in the lounge. Eyes turned as Zelda entered, she always had this effect on people. 'Hello Donald,' she said evenly, as he rose and indicated that she should join him on the sofa. 'No I prefer this chair, thank you.'

Let us establish right away that the days of him telling me what to do are over, she thought.

'Would you like anything, a drink or tea?' Donald asked.

'No thank you, let us get this over as soon as possible. Now what did you want to discuss?'

Donald leaned forward, his face serious. 'First, why did you run off without telling me? I was going to ask you to marry me when I got back from New York.'

Zelda leaned back in her chair and crossed one elegant leg over the other. 'Funny you decided to ask me at that time, after eight years together. Anyway, my answer would have been no.'

Donald looked shocked. He was used to getting his own way. Zelda felt confident and pleased that she had a chance to tell Donald what she thought. Harrison had been right to say that it would be best to finish things finally.

Donald looked at Zelda as if she was still an employee and continued, 'You are not thinking about this properly. If you give up this romantic Cornish nonsense and your new man, or is it men? I will take you back. I have had a private detective follow you for a while, and he has reported that as well as the chap that I hit last night, you are carrying on with the other guy, the one with the pony tail.'

Zelda laughed at the absurdity of this revelation.

'A detective? You were wasting your money then. Nothing was going on.' Not until last night, she thought smugly, wondering how she had never noticed a private eye following her.

'The truth is Donald, I'm happy living on my own and I have plans for a small project in the future. I have learnt many things about my family and myself since I moved to Cornwall. I know we have had some great times together but you must accept it is over.'

With that, Zelda got up and walked out of the hotel. Sitting in her car before driving away, she sent a text to Harrison.

Donald is history. All OK. Missing you already. Love

x

# CHAPTER 14
# AUTUMN

It was October, the days grew shorter and the evenings were getting dark much earlier. Zelda was seeing Cornwall as a very different place than when she first arrived. There were fewer visitors, less traffic and less to do. A chill wind greeted her on her walks along the beach with the dogs. She shivered in her thin jacket and realised the town clothes she had brought with her were inadequate for the coming winter.

A trip to St Ives was called for and so she was driving along the coast road one more time. The miles of angry sea, with white topped breakers, sped by and her thoughts, as they often did turned to Harrison. He was working in the main office back in London; Zelda had only seen him once since the night of the party, when he came down to supervise retakes for the documentary. They met that evening at the Anchor for a meal and he spent the night at the house with her. The old magic was there but next morning he was off again with only texts to keep in touch.

Arriving in St Ives, Zelda first visited Miles at his Gallery.

'Just the person I wanted to see.' he said, 'I have wonderful news. I sent the two abstract paintings to Christy's in New York and a very wealthy collector has snapped them up. In addition, the other paintings by Tommy are to be auctioned next month and I have been told that there is massive interest in them. When it's all finalised, I can give you a thorough breakdown of the prices. You will be quite the little heiress.'

Zelda beamed at Miles, 'That's great; I'm on a shopping trip to buy warm winter togs so I won't feel guilty if I go a bit mad. You certainly know your contacts, I wouldn't have known where to start without you.'

Miles laughed and said. 'Horses for courses, I've been in this lark for a long time, I should know what I am doing. How are you getting on? Jenny says you are going out with the guy who took the punch on the jaw at your party.'

Zelda nodded, 'Yes that's true, only he lives in London, so it's a bit of a long distance romance.'

Miles looked concerned, 'Not a good situation for you. Find a local boy. That's what I tell my girls but it mostly falls on deaf ears.'

Zelda smiled at him, 'I'll carry on looking. Now I mustn't keep you any longer. Bye Miles and thank you.'

Miles held the door open for her, 'Look after yourself, happy shopping.' he said, watching her stride away down the cobbled street.

It was easy to spend money in the town; there were lovely sensible clothes stocked in the small, but classy shops. Only stopping for a coffee and a buttered teacake, Zelda arrived back at the house and unloaded her horde of neatly packed carrier bags. Upstairs she inspected her purchases. Two thick jumpers, a quilted, belted jacket, a long waterproof coat, two pairs of boots, three scarves and a couple of pull on knitted hats. I could get a job as a roving outside TV reporter, the ones they send to cover floods and cold weather crisis. She thought somewhat cynically.

That evening Jenny had invited Zelda and Patti for a girly evening. After a meal of vegetable lasagne, salad and garlic bread, washed down with chilled white wine, they sat by the fire chatting comfortably. First, the talk turned to Mad Iris, as she was still referred to, in spite of her change of identity.

'Hawke Hall has been sold because Iris appeared not to have any relatives,' Jenny reported, 'it needs massive repairs after the fire so it was sold for a knock down price although the identity of the purchaser isn't known. The money will go towards keeping Iris in a good retirement home; it appears she was quite wealthy anyway.'

Zelda leaned forward, 'I wonder who has bought it? As they will be my neighbour, I don't want another nut case next to my house. We were lucky that the fire didn't spread. If there had been a high wind, who knows what could have happened.'

Jenny took a sip of wine, 'All I know is it's someone local, she said, 'have you any plans Zelda?'

It was nice being asked, Zelda thought. She wanted to bounce an idea she had been mulling over, to Jenny and Patti to get their reactions.

'Well,' she said, 'I must do something to keep me occupied and I was thinking of opening a teashop at home.'

Patti's eyes widened with surprise, 'What in the house'? she queried.

'No, I would convert the conservatory. It was big enough when we had the party for quite a crowd and that was when the idea came to me. This would only be from May to the end of October. I would put tables and umbrellas in the garden and if it rained, we could use the conservatory. So many cars pass or stop to go to the beach and there is nowhere for a snack or a coffee. I know there is the Anchor pub; however, a teashop would be more family friendly. What do you think?'

Jenny considered this thoughtfully, 'I reckon it's worth a go,' she said, 'Patti what do you think? As you were in catering, you have experience in that field.'

This was news to Zelda, 'Have you?' she queried excitedly, 'perhaps we could join forces, as apart from eating in them I have no idea how to set up a teashop.'

Patti smiled at her, 'Before my divorce I used to run a hotel with my ex-husband and I've been looking for something to do for quite some time.'

Jenny laughed, 'What will you call it, Bored Ladies Caff?'

Zelda thought for a moment then said, 'No, Tommy's Teas.'

'I think he would like that,' Jenny said approvingly.

Zelda felt excited by the revelation that Patti had previous experience in the catering world and decided not to hang about. 'How do you feel about forming a company?' she asked, 'I have the ideal site and you have the knowhow, we could start in a small way and if the interest is there, we'll be able to expand. How are you fixed for time?'

Patti thought for a minute before replying. 'Let's strike while the iron's hot, I can come round tomorrow afternoon.'

They both smiled happily and Jenny had to admit she felt slightly left out.

'You two are going to be really busy,' she said, 'I suppose I can always do the washing up.'

Zelda shook her head and said, 'No way, we have a big dish washer and my house is a no washing up by hand area.'

Changing the subject Jenny asked about Harrison. 'Is lover boy still around?'

Zelda visibly glowed. 'I've had a lot of texts from him, however he's terribly busy as his documentary is about to be screened on television this week. In fact, he's being interviewed on the morning news programme tomorrow for a bit of publicity.'

Jenny and Patti squealed excitedly, 'fancy knowing a famous TV personality,' they chorused. 'I'll record it,' Patti said. 'then we can show it to everyone who misses seeing it live.'

After another half an hour catching up with events, Patti and Zelda thanked Jenny for a lovely evening and departed their various ways.

Next morning Zelda turned on the television. After a few news items the presenter introduced Harrison.

'Tonight is the first part of a documentary about Cornwall and its history,' she said, 'we are lucky enough to have Harrison de Ville, the producer and director of the series with us. Now Harrison, tell us what we can expect?'

Harrison was relaxed, concise and relayed the outline of the programme with charm and humour. Zelda noted that the female presenter was all smiles and her body language showed she found him very attractive. Harrison's lovely warm voice came over well, in fact better than the presenter's, who annoyingly tended to swallow the end of a sentence, leaving the viewer losing place names.

'So you will be the narrator of the series then?' the female Anchor asked.

Harrison smiled at her and she visibly melted into girly confusion. 'We always use a local actor. I have had a lot of help from people who live in those parts and I really love the area. The views are stunning and the history of the smuggling, fishing and tin mines we found extremely interesting.'

Zelda thought Harrison had just the right look for television. Jeans with tan suede boots and a pale blue cashmere Jumper, that brought out the blue of his eyes. Clever boy, she thought or perhaps he had taken advice from a stylist.

'Is there a follow up project you have lined up, Harrison?' the presenter enquired.

'Well, we are thinking of Norfolk for our next series. It also has a fascinating history and some very famous people came from there, but nothing is finalised as yet.' Harrison smiled at the camera; the presenter thanked him and introduced the next item.

Norfolk, Zelda thought that would mean he is further away than ever.

The phone rang and it was Patti. 'Didn't he do well?' she said.

'Wonderful, the boy has talent.' Zelda replied, but somehow felt the first stirrings of disquiet. 'I'll see you later Patti, bye.'

It was nearly Christmas. The first snow had fallen and Zelda was glad of the big open grates in the two reception rooms in addition to the central heating. Cador had arrived with a large supply of logs that he said had come from a property he had been working at, and that she would be doing him a favour taking them.

'That will be lovely, now I'll be as warm as toast. In fact, I'll toast muffins on a long toasting fork when the fire is really hot. It's years since I did that. You are a real sweetie Cador.'

Cador shrugged and with his customary twinkle said, 'yeah, yeah, well it seems it's the only way I can keep you warm.'

Zelda laughed, 'you never give up do you? What's the local gossip? Who's bought Hawke Hall?'

'Still a mystery,' he replied, 'but there is a lot of work going on up there. Have you heard from your cashmere jumper-wearing boyfriend recently? We poor Cornish yokels can only afford scratchy, rough wool.'

Zelda ignored the jibe at Harrison and replied. 'Well, actually Harrison is coming down this weekend to close the office and studio in St Ives. Apparently the head honcho has decided that now the Cornish documentary is completed they no longer need a base here and are going to do everything from the London Headquarters.'

Cador looked concerned, 'I'm sorry because that means you'll not be seeing much of him. Still as they say, the path of true love never did run smooth. Anyway I must push on as I have a lot to do,' and with a cheery wave he was off.

'Thanks.' Zelda called after him.

# CHAPTER 15
# MOVING ON

Harrison had asked Zelda to meet him in St Ives at the same restaurant by the harbour that she had been to with Jenny. As she arrived, Harrison was waiting outside. After kissing her warmly, they went inside and were shown to a table by the window.

Once seated Zelda gazed at Harrison thinking how handsome he was but also noting the exhaustion lines traced on his face and a certain sadness in those riveting blue eyes.

'Are you OK?' she queried, 'have you been working too hard?'

Harrison laughed. 'Now don't Mother Hen me darling. I suppose I have been very busy. The documentary about Cornwall has been shortlisted for the television awards ceremony, and so I have been doing the rounds of interviews. Answering all those questions can be exhausting but I'm still quite excited.'

Zelda nodded, 'Well they must think you have done a good job. Why are they shutting the studio and office here in St Ives then?'

'Cut backs, they tell me. Everything will now be from our London premises. In addition, they have promoted me and I'm supposed to be nearer to the centre of things. Of course, I will still be out doing documentaries like the next one in East Anglia but that's not far from London. Unfortunately, it means I won't be able to see so much of you.'

Zelda felt a cold chill and shivered, was this the end of their romance? She stared at Harrison feeling tears start to fill her eyes. Blinking hard and hoping he had not noticed she said lightly.

'Well you could always whisk me off to some distant spot for a holiday or something else.' What she meant was something permanent. I'm unattached and you said your marriage is over, but it was impossible to read Harrison's mind, his face was inscrutable.

Just then, the waiter came up and the moment passed as they gave him their orders. Zelda had lost her appetite but ordered a crab salad, which she pushed unenthusiastically round her plate while Harrison made short work of his salmon.

After a while Harrison took her hand and said, 'You know I think the world of you but we are both grownups and I'm afraid my career must come first. If I threw it all up now, all that I have worked for would be wasted, you do understand darling don't you?'

Zelda wanted to say that she did not. That she wanted him with her always. She wanted to make a childish scene but instead she forced a smile and said, 'Well perhaps one day things will change. Meanwhile I will press on with my plan to open the teashop with Patti.'

'I know you will make it a success.' Harrison said seriously. 'There's a real need for somewhere like that in the area. I would have loved to be able to have a quiet cup of tea or coffee then sit, and read a paper when I was first checking for locations. Keep the daily newspapers available for customers to read, that's very civilised and like the Americans do, offer customers free refills of coffee.'

'Hmm, good advice, I hadn't thought of that.' Zelda said standing up and putting on her coat. 'Shall we have a stroll round the town?'

After leaving the restaurant, they wandered along hand in hand and when passing a jeweller's shop Harrison stopped and looked in the window. 'You don't wear rings do you?' he said. 'Let's go in and have a look.'

Inside he asked to look at a special tray from the window display. Choosing one with a square cut emerald in the centre and a large diamond either side, he passed it over to Zelda.

Which finger she thought as she hesitated, he took it from her and placed it on the ring finger of her right hand. It sparkled and looked wonderful. But Zelda had hoped he would put it on her left hand.

'A perfect fit.' Harrison said to the Jeweller, 'we'll take it.'

'Oh Harrison,' Zelda gasped, 'it's far too expensive.'

'Not for a classy bird like you.' he laughed, producing his credit card.

'Shall I put it in a box?' The assistant enquired.

'No my girlfriend will wear it.' Harrison replied.

Ah so that's who I am Zelda thought. Not a fiancée, not a partner, not his intended, just his girlfriend. But she took his arm as they left the shop and whispered, 'That was a lovely surprise, I will wear it every day and think of you.'

'This is goodbye for now then.' Harrison said sadly, giving her a hug and a lingering kiss. 'I will phone when I can.'

'Yes, please phone me and let me know how you are getting on.' Zelda was surprised her voice sounded so normal when all she could think of was that she had no idea when they would next be together again. As she walked away, the feeling of finality hit her and the unshed tears splashed down her face.

The following day Miles arrived at the house after first phoning to check Zelda would be in.

'It's good news' he said smiling broadly, 'the sale of the pictures and memorabilia in America are complete and were an enormous success. It seems Tommy still has a vast amount of fans who remember him and the group. Prices went through the roof and passed all the estimates. I have a cheque here for an eye-watering amount. If you invest this wisely you will be comfortable for life.' With that, he handed Zelda a brown envelope that contained an itemized account and a cheque clipped to the top. After reading the amount of money printed on the cheque, she gasped and sat down on the sofa.

'Miles you are a genius,' she said, 'thank you so much for handling this for me. Tommy, in a roundabout way has looked after me, even if it is after he is dead. I'll use some of this money to set up the teashop and get advice on the best way to invest the remainder. Life is full of surprises and this last year has been a corker.'

Miles smiled at her. 'You deserve a bit of luck, life has not always been easy I suspect. Karen and I have always been around to look after our girls, something you have missed out on, so I'm glad at last you have some security. By the way Karen says that if you don't yet have plans for Christmas day will you join us at our house?'

'I would love to,' Zelda said, 'it's a long time since I had a family Christmas.'

After a cup of coffee, Miles drove off back to St Ives. Zelda took the dogs for their walk on the beach, still marvelling at her change of fortune and planning how to set up the teashop.

Christmas day at Miles and Karen's house turned out to be a good old-fashioned one. A huge turkey with all the trimmings, followed by Christmas pudding and brandy sauce, then a choice of liquors and much laughter.

Following the meal, the three girls insisted that Miles and Karen sit and watch the Queen's message on the television while they washed up.

'This will ruin my nails.' Patti said, as she stood with her hands in the soapy water. 'Mum's priceless dinner service has been in our family for years and we are told never to put it in the dishwasher. I much prefer the thick every-day china that one can just shove in the dishwasher and let it do the work.'

'When we order the crockery for our teashop,' said Patti, 'we'll make sure it's all dishwasher proof.' Zelda agreed.

'After the New Year we'll get all the catalogues and order everything we are going to need. I'm going to get Cador to make the waste ground at the side of the house into an additional car park. I checked the plans of the property the other day and that piece of ground belongs to Marryat House.' said Zelda.

'I feel quite envious of you two', Jenny sighed, 'in my job all I get is coughing kids and endless rheumaticky joints.'

Patti laughed, then noticing Zelda's hand as she picked up another plate to dry, gasped and said, 'Wow, where did you get that ring? I've never seen you wearing it before.'

'Harrison bought it for me when he last came down.'

'Does that mean you have an understanding then?'

Zelda looked at the ring sparkling on her finger. 'I wish.' she said, 'Unfortunately Harrison's career seems to come before me at the moment. Perhaps after the television awards are over I can talk him into something more permanent.'

'You and Jenny always seem to get slippery boyfriends who won't commit,' Patti said, 'while I've been married twice and both times it was a disaster. I don't know which is worse.'

Miles came into the kitchen. 'Come on girls, cheer up. Who's going to take me on for a game of Cluedo?'

After that, it was Poker and then ham sandwiches followed by Christmas cake. Finally, Zelda said she must get back. 'I haven't enjoyed myself so much for ages. Thank you for a lovely day.' she said.

It was quite true, driving back, she thought how lucky Jenny and Patti were to have such lovely parents.

On New Year's Eve, Zelda met Jenny and Patti at the Anchor. It was noisy and jolly with most of the regulars there. As midnight struck, Cador did the rounds, kissing all the girls. When he came to Zelda, she was surprised that she only got a quick peck on the cheek.

Emboldened by a glass of bubbly she said, 'Not up to your usual standard, I suspect Cador.'

'Saving it for another day Princess.' he grinned and moved on to the next lucky lady.

Joe and Mrs joe came up and clinked glasses. 'Happy New Year, Zelda. Did you think a year ago that you would be here in a pub in Cornwall?' Joe said.

'Never,' she replied, 'but I'm so glad I am and life is far more interesting. I wonder what this coming year will bring'

'Whatever it is, good luck.' They said moving on.

Zelda went back to join the girls at their table. 'As we are all walking back we have got you another drink. Here's to us.' Jenny said raising her glass and they joined in singing a rather slurred version of Auld Langsyne.

The night of the television awards Zelda sat down on the sofa to watch. It all looked very glamourous and the show started with the best drama award and progressed through the other categories, until eventually it reached the documentary nominations. There were three mentioned, one highly fancied, was about wild life in Borneo. Another told the history of the Great Wall of China.

'Get on with it,' muttered Zelda leaning forward like an excited child.

'Finally,' the compere said, 'we come to a riveting documentary about the history of life in the lovely, wild county of Cornwall.'

There followed some fascinating shots of familiar places with a well-known actor intoning the accompanying script. The compere opened the gold envelope and announced.

'The winner is.... "A History of Cornwall".'

The camera swung to one of the round tables where eight people were seated. There were three young looking men and one older man. Two girls, who were smiling ecstatically and a very sophisticated, dark haired, slightly older woman seated next to Harrison. They all jumped up cheering and clapping. The woman flung her arms round Harrison and kissed him. After disentangling himself, Harrison, smiling broadly, made his way up to the stage and took the award. The speech he made was just right. Thanking his team and mentioning the camera operator. Also saying how he had enjoyed the hospitality and help of the people he had met while on location in the area.

'Too true.' Zelda thought cynically but was puzzled as to whom the people were at his table, especially the woman who gave off such an air of familiarity.

'I really know nothing about him.' she said stroking Henry who had come up to her after recognising Harrison's voice.

It was true. All she knew was what Harrison had told her of his life when he was back in London. 'I'm too trusting and go where my heart leads me. Next time I see Harrison I will ask lots of questions.' Turning off the television, Zelda said goodnight to the two dogs and went up to bed. Sleep was a long time coming as she dwelt on what was the connection between Harrison and the dark haired woman.

The next few weeks flew by as Zelda and Patti ordered all the equipment and garden furniture that they thought they would need for the teashop. As things arrived, they piled up in the conservatory waiting to be unpacked.

Zelda phoned Cador and asked him to come and see her. 'I would like you to give me an estimate to make a car park on the piece of waste ground next to the house please.' She said when he arrived.

Cador fixed her with his usual quizzical stare. 'How quickly do you want it?' he said 'We are very busy right now.'

'Like yesterday.' she said 'We plan to open in the middle of March and time is whizzing by. I did a rough sketch of what I want and I think it should have a hedge round the perimeter and a gravel surface. What's your estimate of the cost?'

Cador took out his calculator and entered some numbers. 'Well I'm guessing at the exact size but for you Princess I'll drop everything and this is my estimate.'

Zelda took the calculator and could not believe how reasonable the price he quoted was. 'That's great, so OK I accept that, you really are nice to me.'

'Just part of the service.' he grinned and with his usual saucy smile, he turned to go. 'We'll start on Monday before I change my mind and ask for extra fringe benefits other than regular tea and biscuits.'

'Gosh you are cheeky.' Zelda called after him as he walked away.

Already she had arranged for a local firm of brothers to build an outside toilet and washroom by the side of the house. It had meant laying drains and digging foundations but the six brothers had made short work of the undertaking. Two did the manual work, one was a bricklayer, one a plumber, and one an electrician, and one did tiling. The girls were pleased with how well it had turned out.

'We will have to have an official opening.' Patti had giggled 'Who will be the first to do the christening?'

'There's still a lot to do before we are ready for the launch.' Zelda said 'I must find some things to make it personal to Tommy.'

Wondering where else to look, she remembered seeing a load of boxes under the stairs. There amongst all the assorted things that Tommy had stored, were about a dozen long cardboard tubes with lids. Zelda had left them unopened but now curiosity got the better of her as she rooted round. Opening one it contained a rolled up poster advertising a concert for Tommy and his group in America. As Zelda gazed at it in stunned fascination, she recognised a picture of a very young Rick on the drums and standing playing on the keyboards, a tall figure with long curly red hair just like hers. 'That must be Tommy.' she mused. He was handsome and had a certain air of fun and wildness.

'So that confirms what my father looked like.' Zelda gasped to a bewildered Patti. 'I'll get some of these posters framed and they will hang in the conservatory when we open for business.'

At last, she had a proper image of Tommy that she could display even if it was a commercial impression on a poster. Quickly checking the other tubes, she found they all contained similar posters. Some had never been unrolled, while some were dog-eared, and had obviously been used to advertise venues where the group was going to hold concerts. Names of the towns that were next on their tour were printed across them, including Chicago, San Francisco, Philadelphia and even New York.

Patti agreed to take the slightly battered ones to Miles to get them framed and to see if the pristine ones were of any great value. 'I'm seeing Dad this weekend so I'll take them with me and I can ask him what he thinks.'

'Thanks.' Zelda replied. 'It's funny how the more I uncover in this house the more I find out about my roots.'

With the money from the sale in New York safely in her bank account, Zelda had splashed out on furnishing the annexe over the garage. As well as having specially designed fitted units and wardrobes installed there were new twin beds. The bed covers and matching curtains had big, pink and green flowers dotted over them, the green the exact colour of the carpet. Zelda got a thrill every time she went in the room. It was so bright and pretty.

'A friend from my school days has asked to visit, so I'm sure she will love this room.' she confided to Jenny when she had dropped by for a coffee and Zelda took her upstairs to see how it now looked.

Jenny gazed round, taking in the improvements. 'You are a clever old stick.' She said. 'By the way, Dad was on the phone this morning and he's thrilled with the posters of Tommy and the group. He said to tell you that with luck, the unused ones should sell for a very good price and he will deal with it for you. It's odd because the Tommy we knew here had short grey hair but on those posters as a young man, it was long, red and curly like yours.

Zelda smiled. 'I like that. Now I know where my looks came from. Tommy's colour hair and my mother's colour eyes.'

'That's nice.' Jenny said. 'I hear Maisie's sister is going to be your waitress when you open the tearoom.'

'Yes, that takes the pressure off Patti and me; I'll need time to get the hang of running the kitchen and ordering things. It's a big leap into unknown territory for us and I've had many media enquiries for interviews from Journalists. I think Harrison may have alerted some of his contacts to give us some publicity.'

'He is quite a big fish in that business isn't he?'

Zelda nodded. 'A rather slippery one it seems. How one lands him is beyond me.'

Jenny laughed and looked at her watch. 'Help I am running late, I have to cover for the other nurse, who is on holiday, must fly. Thanks for the coffee.' With that, she hugged Zelda and ran down the stairs.

# CHAPTER 16
# THE TEASHOP

The day of the opening of the teashop came a week before Easter.  At ten o'clock Patti and Hedra, the sister of Maisie, were ready for customers.  The kitchen surfaces groaned with an array of tempting scones and teacakes, plus the option of more filling snacks, no customers yet were sitting at the outside tables or in the conservatory.

Zelda was being interviewed on the local television by a rather new to the job, and nervous female reporter.  The questions were asked in a breathless singsong.  The reporter's name was a jumble of letters that had started out as one thing and trying to be modern, her mother had saddled her with two unpronounceable hyphenated names.

'Call me Flip.' She had said, grabbing her long lank brown hair and pulling it forward over one shoulder. 'I will ask you why you want to open a teashop in Cornwall.'

The interview stumbled on and Zelda found herself taking over. However, that gave her a chance to get the teashop's name in, and promote the fact that all the products they would use, were locally sourced.

'The Cornish cream for our homemade scones is made at farms nearby also the jam that we will use.  A local baker will deliver bread daily so everything will be fresh.  It will take a while to discover what our customers' favourites are, but at this moment, it is all quite fluid.' Zelda smiled at the cameras as Flip thanked her for coming.

'That went well.' Ivan Trevis, the producer said coming up with his IPad at the ready. 'Give me directions, and in a week or so perhaps we can come and film an item of your teashop in action'

'Of course, just give me a call before you come.' Zelda said shaking his hand and smiling broadly as she left him and an overawed Flip.

As she arrived back, there were five cars in the new car park. 'Hooray, customers.' She whooped, rushing inside to find a flushed Patti manning the grill and a whirling Hedra delivering teacakes and coffee to the holidaymakers seated at the tables in the garden.

'We've been quite busy.' Hedra said minutes later as she went past with a tray piled high with dirty crockery on her way to the Dishwasher. 'A man was saying, It's just what the area needed as he was here last year and they couldn't find a cup of tea for miles. Isn't that encouraging?'

'Very! well done Hedra.' said a relieved Zelda.

Trade was steady all that opening week and the menu developed to include toasted sandwiches, jacket potatoes with various fillings and Cornish ice cream. On a day when there was the odd shower, and customers took cover in the conservatory, there was much interest in the posters of the young Tommy and the T men. Four large posters now hung in frames on the wall and Zelda was amazed how many people recognised the young musicians performing all those years ago.

Ivan Trevis was as good as his word and following his phone call, he, Flip and a camera crew turned up and filmed a very flattering piece shown on that evening's local TV news programme. It started with the story of how Zelda was the daughter of the founder of a legendry music group, it even made the National News channels the following day.

Later that week Hedra came into the kitchen where Zelda had just put the phone down after giving her order for the next day's bakery delivery, and said a customer had asked to speak to her.

'I'll be out directly.' Zelda said, thinking, not my first complaint I hope.

'She's in the conservatory, very smart and scary, sitting by herself in the far corner.'

As Zelda went into the conservatory and looked round, there was a lone female sitting at a table with just a cup of black coffee in front of her. The high cheek boned, rather hard face looked vaguely familiar. Even though she racked her brains, Zelda couldn't put a name to her. As she approached the table, the woman indicated the empty chair.

'Please sit down, I would like to talk to you.' She said in a very cut glass accent. 'My name is Giselle, I believe you know my husband Harrison.'

Zelda could not believe what she was hearing. 'Husband?' she queried. 'I understood that he was divorced, or in the process of getting divorced.'

'I have stopped proceedings.' Giselle fixed Zelda with a cold stare. 'My father owns the company that employs Harrison and he thinks the world of him. He does not want us to split up. As father wants to retire, he has offered to make the company over to Harrison as long as we stay together.'

Zelda now remembered why Giselle seemed so familiar. She was the woman hugging Harrison at the award ceremony. Giselle was continuing to speak, so with a great effort Zelda dragged her mind back to this nightmare scenario unfolding in front of her, although she was finding it hard to take it in.

'If it was a case of you versus me, you would win.' The icy voice continued. 'However, if it is a case of me and the business, Harrison would choose that over you. Therefore, you lose my dear Zelda. I suggest you carry on playing teashops and leave Harrison alone.' With that, Giselle threw a couple of coins on the table and swept out.

Zelda's legs refused to move and she sat there for several minutes. Her gaze dropped to the opulent ring Harrison had given her at their last meeting. That had obviously been his parting gift. Finally, she got up and went into the kitchen.

'Are you all right?' Patti asked, 'you're deathly pale.'

'I'll tell you later. I'm going to take the dogs on the beach for a run.'

Calling Prince and Henry, Zelda crossed the road and ran down to the beach. She had to be alone, had to think about this latest blow and needed to try to work out what to do next.

The dogs were running ahead when suddenly Prince staggered and fell on to the sandy beach. 'Prince, what is it?' Zelda called running up and throwing herself down beside his still form. Henry stood whimpering beside her, unsure what had happened. Pulling her phone from her jacket pocket Zelda rang Cador. When he answered, Zelda sobbed. 'Please come to the beach. I think Prince is dead.'

'On my way.' Cador replied.

Within minutes, his Land Rover appeared on the road above the beach. Seconds later, he was beside her and the lifeless form lying stretched out on the sand.

'Sorry Zelda, he's gone.' Cador said after bending down and feeling Prince's chest.

As he stood up Zelda collapsed into his arms unable to stand this latest blow. She had loved Prince and she loved Harrison, however within the last hour it had transpired they both would not be in her life any more. It was too much; she cried hot tears, not caring about anything but how sad she felt.

'You poor little thing.' Cador murmured into her hair, 'but Prince was getting on and I'm sure he didn't know anything about it. I would think he had a heart attack.'

After a while, Zelda pulled herself together and stood back. 'Sorry, I think I made your jumper all wet.' She manged to say.

Cador smiled at her. 'Don't worry about that, it's hardly ever dry. Now you take Henry home, as he looks bewildered. My brother is up there in the car, so we'll follow with poor old Prince and you can decide what you want us to do with him.'

Zelda nodded and calling Henry, she trudged away and up the cliff path. Avoiding the kitchen, she went round into the garden. It wasn't long before Cador and his younger brother, Daniel arrived to join her.

'Show us where you would like Prince buried and then leave it to us.' Cador said. 'We'll let you know when it is time and we can give him a small funeral.'

Zelda thought for a minute and then walked up to a sunny spot at the end of the garden where Prince had liked to sit. 'I think here, I can see it from the house and later on I will get a sundial to mark the spot.'

She turned her gaze to Cador. What a strong person he was. Whenever I'm in trouble, he's the first person I turn to, she thought. Henry obviously thought the same as he was leaning against Cador who was gently stroking his head.

'Off you go then; we'll call you when we've finished.' With that, the two tall men walked back to their car and returned with spades while Zelda went into the kitchen to tell Patti and Hedra the sad news, and to explain about the unwelcome customer.

'You mean that was Harrison's wife?' A flabbergasted Patti exclaimed. 'How did she know about you and where you lived?'

'I would think from the interview I gave on the television, and no doubt she has been looking at Harrison's mobile phone without him knowing. She looked the type. But I truly believed he was unattached when we first met. In all honesty, I think Harrison thought the same. '

'Will you tell him what you think of him?' Hedra said.

'Do you know? I think in my bones I knew nothing would come of our relationship. As they say in the song, "It was great fun but it was just one of those things". I will miss my lovely Prince more, as we had been together since he was a six-week old puppy.'

Patti thrust a cup of very strong tea in to Zelda's hand. 'You look like you could do with this.' she said. 'Two shocks in one day, is not good.'

'Thanks, let's hope the old saying, that things come in threes, isn't true.' Zelda said, helping herself to a readymade cheese sandwich, and the girls were glad to see her normal colour return.

Later as Cador and Daniel lowered the blanket covered shape into the hole they had dug, Zelda gripped Patti's hand and blew a kiss towards it, unable to speak. Then blinded by tears she stumbled back to the house.

No third shock happened that day, in fact it was only good news. After adding up the takings for the first couple of weeks since the teashop opened and deducting expenses, there remained a healthy profit. Later Miles rang up to say the unopened posters she had found under the stairs had sold in New York for top prices and a big cheque would be coming her way. If things kept this busy in the teashop, she would soon recover the cost of setting it up. I'm a woman of independent means Zelda thought. Still she couldn't get Harrison out of her mind. Was making documentary films worth being tied in a loveless marriage?

The weeks flew by, June was hot and sunny, trade was brisk, and Patti's homemade lemonade proved a winner. July and August saw people waiting for tables to be vacated while happy families came and went, refreshed on their way to the beach or to other destinations up the coast.

'Girls we are a big success,' Zelda said, 'the Local paper has printed an article about us. It's headed, "Local Teashop Wows Visitors", now that is praise indeed.'

'Super,' Patti remarked, 'and the other good thing is with all the running around I have lost loads of weight.'

'Me too,' said Hedra, 'I've even had to buy a belt to keep my jeans up.'

The next day an invitation arrived in the post. Opening it Zelda read:

THE NEW OWNER OF HAWKE HALL INVITES YOU TO A RECEPTION ON 1st OCTOBER. CHAMPAGNE AND CANAPES AT 2.30pm.

Well that was a surprise. All summer with the continual work going on at the Hall, there had been speculation everywhere as to the identity of the new owner. Opinions ranged from a famous film star, to a Russian Oligarch.

When Patti and Hedra arrived for work that morning, they were in a great state of excitement.

'We've had invitations to the reception at the Hall,' they chorused, 'and so has Jenny.'

'And so have I.' Zelda said.

Then seeing the practical side of things added, 'We'll have to close the teashop on that day. It's too good to miss.'

'I must buy a new dress; it sounds like this is going to be the event of the year.' Hedra said, 'and I must get my hair done.'

'Jolly exciting.' Patti concurred, 'How about you Zelda. Fancy a snazzy new outfit to dazzle us all?'

'You bet! I'll trawl through the designer collections on the internet and choose some smart number. We've all had our noses to the grindstone this summer so we're due for a treat.'

Customers were arriving so it was back to work. However, there was a spring in their step and many ready smiles that day.

The day of the reception at the Hall arrived and for the first time since the teashop opened, Zelda hung the CLOSED signs up outside. The arrangement was that Jenny and Patti would drive to Zelda's, and that the three of them would walk up to the Hall.

In the morning, after walking Henry on the beach, Zelda had a leisurely shower and washed her hair. Standing in front of the mirror, she noticed that like the girls, she looked slimmer and in good shape. After taking the new dress off the hanger, she slipped it over her head and stood back. Yes, that had been a good choice. It was a white organza maxi dress with a design of tiny flowers dotted over it. Strapless but with a leaf green fitted satin jacket that matched the colour of the belt. It had caught her eye on the screen of her laptop, as it reminded her of Scarlett O'Hara's dress at the start of the film, "Gone with the Wind". Her hair had dried naturally and was a mass of tumbling curls. High green strappy sandals and her mother's real, pearl necklace completed her look.

At two o'clock Jenny and Patti arrived. Both resplendent in new dresses. 'We look like we're off to Ascot races not a Cornish get together.' Jenny giggled as they started walking up the road towards the Hall.

When they arrived, they were amazed at how grand it all looked. The approach to the house was lined with an avenue of trees. A flight of wide stone steps led up to the front door with tall, colonnades either side. The door was open and inside there was already a throng of people gathered, some Zelda knew and some she didn't.

A very imposing man, who looked like a butler bowed as they entered and asked their names.

'Please go through, Madame.' he said to each of them after checking their names off a long list.

'Golly this is impressive.' Patti said, gazing round the entrance hall. It was oak panelled and hung with ancient portraits of fierce looking men in velvet jackets, britches and tall boots. While the portraits of ladies, showed impressive bosoms, straining to escape from low cut brocade dresses that were designed to show off their attributes. Beside the portraits were several pairs of crossed swords hanging over heraldic shields. Underneath, standing at intervals, were dark, carved statues of Nubian men, each one as tall as an average man of today.

As the three girls walked into the main reception room, the sound of music floated down from a string quartet playing in the Minstrel gallery. Waitresses stood with trays of Champagne and others were passing among the guests with a bewildering array of canapés.

'Delicious,' said Hedra, trying a finger of toast topped with Caviar. 'I've never had this before. Who do you think is paying for all this?'

Zelda stared round at the crowd of people also enjoying the exquisite food and chatting away. 'Well I can't see a film star or a Russian with snow on his boots, so your guess is as good as mine.' she said as they laughed at the thought.

'Hello girls, looks like you are enjoying your selves or is it the Champagne?' Cador and Daniel came up to join them, glasses of sparkling Champagne in their hands.

'Just seeing how the other half live.' Jenny smiled up at Daniel who winked down at her.

'It's changed a bit since Mad Iris lived here.' Daniel, who had his brother's dark brooding good looks, said in his soft Cornish accent. He had always fancied Jenny and lived in hope that perhaps one day they would get together.

'My, you both look extra smart today.' Patti remarked, taking in the up to the minute suits and shirts they were wearing.

Cador smiled at her, fixing her with his dark, wicked eyes. 'We scrub up well.' He joked. 'Come on Daniel, let's see if there's any food left before these girls have it all.' With that, the two brothers moved on. Smiling and chatting, their heads visible above most in the room.

Zelda gazed after Cador, wishing he had spent more time with them. He had hardly glanced at her, and for some reason, she wished he had said she looked nice. I suppose I've rebuffed him so many times he doesn't bother with me anymore, she thought.

'Penny for them' Jenny said noting her look, 'have you got over Harrison yet?'

'Yes I have.' Zelda said, suddenly surprised at how true that was. 'After the visit from his ever loving, I really am just sorry for him. Fancy being tied to that woman for the rest of his life. He had a chance to escape and chose to be a wimp. I like strong men.'

'Like those two.' Jenny said, looking at the retreating brothers, 'they're tough boys.'

There was no time to answer as the Master of Ceremonies tapped his glass and started to speak.

'Ladies and Gentlemen, I would like to introduce the new owner of Hawke Hall.'

You could have heard a pin drop as the large crowd stood silent. Then Cador stepped forward to join him.

'Mr Cador Holmes.' The MC finished, stepping back.

There was an audible gasp. No one had expected this. Cador smiled round obviously delighted. 'First of all thank you all for coming. I grew up in this part of Cornwall and always knew that many years ago this house had belonged to my ancestors. We owned it up to the middle of the fifteenth century. However, at that time, The Prayer Book Rebellion raged and unfortunately, the house was taken from us. Over the centuries, Hawke Hall has had a chequered history, although I don't believe all the many tales of smugglers and wreckers living here.

Last year there was a disastrous fire and the house was badly damaged.  When it came up for sale, I offered to purchase and restore Hawke Hall to its former glory.  I am delighted that it is now back with my family.  You may have noticed that there are portraits and antiquities all around.  When we had to knock down walls, left unsafe by the fire, we uncovered a couple of secret, bricked up rooms.  They contained treasured possessions that had been hidden away from the enemy.  It is wonderful that these treasures have survived all these years and now are back in their rightful place and show the high position that my family held in the past.

Well, that is almost the happy ending to my story.  I have one more wish on my list but more about that in due course.  Do look round at the garden before you go and thank you all again for coming.'

There was a ripple of applause and everyone started talking and moving towards the garden.

'Well I didn't see that one coming.' Jenny said,

'Nor me.' echoed Patti, 'How about you Zelda?'

'Flabbergasted.'  Zelda acknowledged. 'I bet he puts his prices up now.'

'Talking about me?   Cador said, coming up to the three girls.

Zelda blushed, furious at being caught discussing him, but he was laughing at her.   'Yes I must revise my charges now that I have a house to keep up. Thank you Jenny and Patti, for coming'. Cador kissed them both on the cheek.

'Zelda, can I show you the Orangery? I'm so pleased with how it has turned out' With that, Cador took her hand, led the way through the vast cavern of the reception area, past the dining room with its long table and dark, ornate sideboard, and into the big glass walled Orangery. It was cool and the scent of many blooms hung heavy in the air. The ceiling rose high above their heads. Below ranged tubs filled with exotic trees, bushes and flowering shrubs of every description. Cador stopped and faced her, his expression, serious for once.

'Darling Zelda I have done all this for you. Do you know it is exactly a year to the day since you first came into the Anchor pub and that's why I chose today to open the Hall?'

Zelda went to speak but Cador said quietly. 'Darling please let me finish. I made up my mind then that you were the only girl for me. I've tried to steer you through the many rocky paths on which you landed. I gather that Harrison is history now and you have proved you can stand on your own two feet. However, let me look after you from now on. What I'm trying to say is will you marry me? Oh and by the way you look stunning in that dress.'

Zelda laughed, the tension of the moment disappeared like a feather in the wind. 'You knew I wanted you to say that, you just love teasing me and yes I would love to marry you.'

Cador took a ring out of his pocket; it had an enormous solitary diamond glinting in the centre. He slipped it on the ring finger of her left hand. It looked wonderful, and sparkled in the late afternoon sun.

'Thank you, I love it.' Zelda said, standing on tiptoe to kiss him. It was their first real kiss and it was magic. Her legs went weak and she would have fallen, if it were not for his strong arms around her.

# CHAPTER 17
# EXCITING TIMES

The next morning when Patti and Hedra arrived for work at the front door of Marryat House it remained shut, despite them ringing the bell repeatedly. Then Cador's Land Rover roared up and they could see Zelda kissing the driver goodbye before jumping out and running up the path.

'What have you got to say for yourself, my girl?' Patti said in mock disapproval. 'Arriving here still wearing yesterday's party frock. You have obviously spent the night in wild abandon.'

A beaming Zelda turned her hand over to show the diamond engagement ring Cador had given her, both girls gasped.

'Not another diamond ring. How do you do it?' Hedra said. 'No one has ever given me a ring. Where do I go wrong?'

'Patience sweetie, I've had a long wait for Mr Right to turn up. Your time will come.'

'Mr Right?' Patti's eyebrows could not have arched any higher. 'Don't tell me someone has nobbled the elusive Cador at last. Mind you, we all knew he was mad about you, only you always gave him the frosty treatment.'

'Well I was an idiot; however, I now realise that he is the one for me. Sorry to keep you waiting, we had better start work before the customers turn up.' With that, still beaming, she unlocked the door and they trooped inside.

Later that morning during a lull from rushing around dealing with customers, Zelda called Patti and Hedra into the kitchen and gave them a glass of Champagne.

'You have been both wonderful to me and I would like you to wish me luck and will you be my bridesmaids?'

'You bet! I will be thrilled, cheers.' Said Patti, raising her glass.

'Me too, good luck.' Hedra was beaming ear to ear.

'Great, I'll ask Jenny as well. Cador and I have said we want a Spring wedding, so lots of planning ahead.'

A car could be heard arriving so they drained their glasses and returned to work, but Zelda saw a worried look on Patti's face.

'Patti, after we close can we have a talk about things.' she said.

'Of course.' Patti replied, giving her a hug.

It had been a quiet day in the teashop. Autumn was blowing the leaves off the trees and by four o'clock the last car had driven out of the car park. Zelda told Hedra she could go home then Zelda and Patti sat down in the conservatory, each with a cup of builder's strength tea.

'I know my news came as a bit of a shock this morning,' Zelda began, 'but this has all happened so suddenly and I had no idea I would finish up being swept of my feet and engaged. I've told Cador I will not move into Hawke Hall until after we are married, I want to do everything the old fashioned way. Not to say we will not share a bed in his place or mine. You and I started the teashop together and it has been a real success, however, I cannot see me being able to continue after I'm married, I've had another idea for a business. Let me run this past you as the saying goes and see what you think.'

Patti nodded, thinking it was great to see Zelda glowing with happiness but from her own point of view she was disappointed that the teashop was going to be so short lived.

Zelda leaned forward looking excited. 'I shall obviously move out of here once we are married and Cador will leave his house in the village. As Tommy left me this house, I could never sell it. Rather than go to an agency to let them both I thought that we could start our own agency for short holiday lets. We have so many rooms at the Hall we could use one of them as an office and with a computer, printer and phone in there and of course a desk and chairs, that would be all we would need. I've noticed several houses round here left empty while people with properties abroad, are away for the summer. I am sure the owners would jump at the chance to let them provided they were managed properly. What do you think?'

'Yes that could be a nice little business and with minimal overheads. Would Hedra be included? She's as bright as a button.'

'Of course, you would need one of you to be in the office while the other one would be out checking properties and showing customers round. I would be on hand to cover for days off and busy periods.'

'I'm happy with that, Is Cador in agreement?'

'Of course, I asked him and he says as long as I'm kept amused he's fine with the idea. We still have several weeks of the teashop being open, as we always said we would close for the winter at the end of October.'

Patti smiled and said,          'You certainly have him where you want him.  I really must go now as I need a shower, and do ask Jenny about being a bridesmaid soon, as I'll not be able to keep quiet about you and Cador for long.'

'The minute you go I'll be on the phone to her.  Gosh, this has been a riveting couple of days.'

After Patti left, Zelda phoned Jenny who whooped with delight when Zelda gave her the news, and then agreed to be a bridesmaid.

'No black, navy or red for our dresses please,' she said, 'and peach does terrible things to my complexion.'

'OK, got the message.' Zelda laughed, 'This is going to be a very traditional wedding, I fancy pink for the bridesmaids' dresses and long, pink gloves.  How does that sound?'

'Fine,    can't    wait.'    A    relieved    Jenny    said. 'Congratulations to you and Cador, I couldn't be more pleased.  Bye for now.'

When Cador arrived a bit later, Zelda ran down the stairs and hurled herself at him while Henry did the same.

'What a welcome.' he laughed. 'How I've missed you both and that's just since this morning.'

'Let's take Henry for a walk on the beach before supper.  I've put a lasagne in the oven so we have plenty of time.' Zelda smiled adoringly at Cador who said, 'I can't believe this is happening.'

'Neither can I, everyone I've told today is delighted.' she said putting on her dog-walking jacket. 'Walkies first, then food, and I want to talk weddings and guest lists.'

'What have I got myself into?' Cador groaned in pretend horror, but he winked at her as they crossed the road hand in hand.

On the beach, Henry ran up with a piece of wood he'd found and dropped it at Caldor's feet then looked up at him wanting a game. 'OK, fetch.' Cador said, throwing the wood as far as possible. Henry retrieved it and brought it back, looking up at Cador asking for more.

'He really loves you,' Zelda said happily, 'but do you realise I hardly know anything about you. I mean, your family, your hobbies and your past. Did you have an affair with Maisie?'

Cador smiled. 'You mean walking off hand in hand with her after your barbeque? No, I like her but that was just to try to make you jealous. Of course at the time you only had eyes for Harrison. Are you going to ask him to the wedding?'

'No way! He might turn up with that scary dragon of a wife of his. Besides now I have you, I realise you are the only one I want to be with for the rest of my life. Harrison would have bored me after a while. Far too arty and driven for me. It has all worked out for the best in the end.'

Zelda tucked her arm in his, and calling Henry, they started to walk back up the beach.

'I nearly bought you a puppy when you lost Prince,' Cador said after a while. 'However, as you were so busy with the teashop I thought it wouldn't be fair to give you more work, puppies take up a lot of time. After we're married, if you like we'll get a puppy to keep Henry company.'

'Thank you darling, what a lucky girl I am.' Zelda sighed as they crossed the road.

After the meal they curled up on the sofa and Zelda said, 'Right tell me about your family, all I've seen so far is Daniel, so what happened to your parents?'

Cador thought carefully for a moment before saying. 'They're both dead. My father had a thriving fishing business here, he owned two quite big boats. When Daniel and I were growing up, we were always out with him in a boat at weekends and during the holidays. One night a big storm blew up and the boat he was skippering was lost. Dad and the two-crew members with him were never found. My mother took his death really badly. That winter she caught influenza and that turned into pneumonia with complications, and she too passed away. I don't think she wanted to go on without him, the last time we saw her in the hospital she made Daniel and I promise that we would never be fishermen. That's why we started the landscaping and market garden businesses after we had both done courses at agricultural college.'

'Oh darling, that is sad. So we're both orphans even though we are grown up.'

'Well I suppose you might say that, however I have aunts, uncles and cousins, so they did keep an eye on us although as the elder brother I've always been very protective and close to Daniel. I would like him to be my Best Man.'

'Of course, you and Daniel are like peas in a pod and the thought of you both in Morning suits is delicious. I've asked Jenny, Patti, and Hedra to be my bridesmaids, and they've said yes. Also, although, I haven't asked him yet, I would like Miles to give me away.'

Cador smiled down at her. 'You have been a busy girl, it's lovely to see you so excited. I expect you're now going to tell me where you want to go on honeymoon.'

'Funny you should say that, I was thinking of the most romantic place we could go to and its Italy. We would take the Hydrofoil from Sorrento to Capri for the day, stay in Rimini and have a thin Pizza, baked in an open oven. See the hanging gardens and buy a Cameo ring in Ravello. Eat lunch on the Amalfi coast, then stay in Venice, where you can kiss me in a Gondola and buy me a peach Bellini at Harry's bar and then stroll to the Bridge of Sighs and finish with coffee and cake in St Mark's Square. Next, on to see Leonardo's statue of David in Florence and visit the museums and art galleries in the town. Then, coffee in the square in Sienna and collapse for a couple of days at the Terme di Montecatini, hot thermal spring Spa. Visit Herculaneum and Pompeii, next, on to Rome to toss a coin in the Trevi Fountain and walk to the Vatican.' Zelda ran out of breath.

Cador laughed. 'Is that it, I'm exhausted already.'

'No there are tons more things that I've not even mentioned yet. I've been to all these places with Donald, but it was to meet and entertain his business associates and I always told myself that if I ever met the right person I would go back with them. It would take a few weeks to do it all. Can we darling?'

'I would love to do all that with you. I've led a very insular life here. The furthest I've been is scuba diving in the Red Sea. Most of my holidays have been spent surfing at beaches around the coast here, mostly Newquay and Porthmeor Beach. '

'Ah, so that's where you get those stunning 6 pack stomach muscles and the Rambo torso.' Zelda sighed happily. 'I noticed that when you first came and did my garden.'

'You were supposed to; I was showing off a bit. But I've made some good friends surfing and as you have your bridesmaids organised, I'll ask several of my surfing chums to be ushers'. Cador yawned. 'What an exhausting day, shall we call it a day and go to bed?'

When Zelda awoke next morning, she smiled as she felt Cador's warm body next to hers and cast a casual eye at the clock on her bedside table, they had overslept. She leant over and kissed his tanned shoulder.

'Darling wake up, we've overslept but we can catch up.' Then grabbing her dressing gown, she ran downstairs and let Henry out into the garden. Back upstairs and pulling on her jeans and a sweater she said. 'What do you like for breakfast?' Thinking how odd, we're engaged to be married and I still don't know much about him.

Cador rolled out of bed and stood up completely in the buff. A fabulous sight Zelda thought, but no time for that now.

'Oh, Eggs Benedict, Lark's Tongues and Devilled Kidneys,'

'Cador be serious. I don't want the girls to arrive and find us...' she tailed off realising Cador could not care less.

'Just toast and tea please Miss, I have the full English only at the weekends.'

As they sat at the breakfast bar in the kitchen, Zelda said as she munched her toast, 'What are you doing today?'

'Daniel and I are laying up the boat for the winter.'

I thought your mother didn't want you to go to sea?'

'This is only a cabin cruiser we use in the summer, not a big fishing boat; it's just to run around in the bay. You can't take the sea out of a Cornish man's blood.'

Zelda poured them both another cup of tea. 'Where do you keep the boat in the winter?'

'In our boatyard, Dad owned the yard, also the Chandlers there and several outbuildings. Daniel and I are converting them into holiday cottages. There's a big empty barn as well, that if you're ever interested we can make into a harbour restaurant.'

This was news to Zelda. 'Darling you are obviously a man of property and not short of a bob or two so why did you come and do my garden? I thought you were just a jobbing gardener with a tale of bigger things.'

Cador gave her one of his devastating naughty boy looks. 'Why do you think? How else was I going to get to know you? We actually employ quite a few people. The market garden supplies hotels and restaurants all around here. You need not ever worry about money, just enjoy yourself, go mad about the wedding.'

'Can I put an announcement in the Times Newspaper?'

'Anything you want Darling but I must be off now, Daniel will be waiting. Meet me in the Anchor tonight and we will have a meal there, does seven suit you?'

Zelda kissed him saying. 'That sounds lovely, golly just in time, I can hear the girls arriving.'

As he was leaving Cador passed Patti and Hedra in the hall.

'Early morning call?' Hedra said, while Patti giggled.

'Just checking the flower beds.' Cador smiled as he walked to his car.

That night when Zelda walked into the Anchor a cheer went up. Cador was already at the bar and obviously, the news of their engagement had travelled fast. One after another, people came up to offer their congratulations. Cador beamed and Zelda said how happy she was at the prospect of becoming Cador's wife.

'About time someone took him in hand, there's been too much sobbing in this pub over our Cador.' The Landlord joked, adding to Zelda, 'I'm really pleased for you both and I understand you first met in here.'

'That's correct, perhaps you can put up a blue plaque to record the event.' she answered smiling broadly.

Then they sat down and tucked into chicken pie and chips washed down with a cold glass of Pinot Grigio. Zelda sipped her wine and looked across the table at Cador saying, 'darling at the opening of Hawke Hall when you were making your speech, you said you had one more wish on your list, what did you mean?'

'That I hoped you would marry me. I think everyone but you knew what I wanted. I had the ring in my pocket, but I didn't know if you would say yes or turn me down.'

'If I had, what would you have done?'

'Oh, asked the next girl I saw, become a monk or die a bitter old bachelor. Come on darling, I really don't know, however, happily, you said yes.'

'I'm so glad you persisted, I really do love you.'

'Good. By the way, Daniel is going to live in Hawke Hall until we get married. He agreed it wasn't good for word to get round that no one was living there. He has a nice flat above the Chandlery by the Harbour, however; it's quite safe to leave that.'

'That's good of him, who will he lure up to the Hall, do you think?'

'Jenny for one if he can. Will you put in a good word for him? That Alvar has rather stolen Daniel's limelight. There are quite a few other girls he's been out with, but Jenny is the one he really likes.'

OK I'll do my best. Jenny is almost like family to me, so if they got together that would be super. I would like her to be as happy as I am.' Zelda smiled dreamily into Cador's dark eyes and with a wave to the Landlord, they left the pub.

At the end of October, the teashop was finally closed for the last time. Zelda felt a pang of regret but then turned her thoughts to more practical matters. Thinning out the spare furniture from the teashop and moving all, but one, of the wooden picnic tables and attached benches to the Hawke Hall garden, made Marryat House a normal home again. Cador and Daniel took down the teashop signs and locked the gate into the car park. As one door closes, another door opens Zelda thought, starting to plan the setting up of the Agency.

Jenny arrived in a great state of excitement to say that she and Patti had booked a three-week Cruise round the Mediterranean. 'After being a crew member, I will now be a passenger and experience a different kind of life on board ship. All that lovely food and entertainment to enjoy.'

'I'm thrilled for you,' Zelda said, 'but on another subject, tell me how do you feel about Daniel, I mean do you like him?'

'I have a real weak spot for him,' Jenny looked quite sad adding, 'however, he's not shown much interest in me since I've lived here.'

'That's because of your boyfriend Alvar.'

'Boyfriend!' Jenny burst out laughing, 'but Alvar is gay, we really are just good friends.'

Zelda's jaw dropped. 'Wait until I tell Daniel that.' she laughed. 'What a shame you're going away just now.'

'We are off tomorrow, so do tell him and when I get back all tanned and relaxed perhaps sparks will fly.'

'I do hope so. Goodbye Jenny, have a lovely time.' Zelda said, walking to the front door with her.

# CHAPTER 18
# CHRISTMAS AND PLANS

The start of Christmas arrived in a flurry of snow and storms. Cador wanted Hawke Hall to be, as no doubt it had once been, the centre of family entertaining, and Zelda thought this was brilliant. Daniel and Jenny were taking tentative steps towards a romance and Jenny accepted the invitation for lunch and the rest of the day. This was all Zelda needed to swing into action. She ordered a big turkey, spent days making lists of menus and even longer ones of the groceries she needed to buy. Taking a leaf out of Mad Iris's book, she ordered hampers of food from the upmarket shop in Truro and these were delivered to the Hall. As Jenny was already coming, Zelda asked Miles, Karen and Patti for the day as well, and they said they would love to come.

Cador joined Daniel and stayed at the Hall on the days leading up to Christmas. They carried an enormous Christmas tree into the hall, which Zelda helped them decorate with lights and baubles. Wrapped parcels for everyone were piled up underneath the tree, and bunches of Mistletoe hung from the big chandeliers.

When everyone was sitting round the beautifully laid table in the dining room on Christmas day, Cador expertly carved the turkey and before they started to eat, he raised his glass. 'A big thank you to everyone for making this a perfect day and a special thank you to my lovely Zelda, who has been busy in the kitchen for days.'

A flushed Zelda gazed round the table at the people she loved best. 'Happy Christmas everyone.' She said, taking a big sip of the vintage wine, thinking life could not get much better.

After the New Year Zelda planned a trip to Truro to buy a wedding dress and dresses for her three bridesmaids. With Jenny, Patti and Hedra on board her big car, they drove off in high spirits.

'As I'm the only one of you to have been married, I will play Mother of the Bride and get all teary when you try on the dresses.' Patti announced.

'No tears on my parade'. Zelda replied, 'I just hope I can find the right one.'

The first shop they tried had some lovely dresses but nothing really stood out. The second had rows of white, cream and even black dresses of every length and design. Selecting three, Zelda went into the dressing room with the assistant. The girls sat sipping sparkling wine while they could hear the sound of zips being done up. When Zelda came out they all gasped, she looked stunning.

'Lovely.' They chorused.

'Try the other two.' The assistant said.

'Zelda would look good in a sack.' Jenny remarked, as Zelda went back into the fitting room.

The second dress raised oo's and ah's but the third one did it.

'That's the one.' Patti said and sure enough, her eyes were misty and so were the others.

'I love it.' Zelda said gazing at her reflection in the full-length mirror. The dress was pure white, with a strapless draped bodice and a skirt that clung to her hips and then fanned out with a small train at the back. When the assistant added a diamante tiara and gossamer veil, the picture was complete. 'Job done.' Zelda smiled, 'now for the bridesmaids' dresses. 'I think pink chiffon with tiny straps.'

Miraculously the exact dress Zelda had described was found and after measuring the girls, an order for three was placed, to be ready in two to three weeks. The shade of soft pink suited all three girls. Hedra had the dark wild look of her ancient Cornish stock. Her hazel eyes had flecks of green in them and were ringed with unbelievably long lashes. Jenny was blonde and curvy, while Patti was also blonde, but with a darker complexion that tanned easily. All of them suited the style of the dress, and with silver high heeled shoes and the long pink gloves Zelda chose they all looked fabulous.

Zelda sighed happily. 'Eighteen months ago I would not have dreamed I would be getting married this Spring, and that I would have three such lovely Bridesmaids.'

Always the one to be down to earth, Patti said, 'Come on before we get too mushy let's get something to eat. I know a pub that serves delicious bar snacks. '

So after Zelda thanked the staff for their help, they all followed Patti out of the shop and found the pub. It proved to be just what they needed and was a very noisy and jolly meal.

On the way home talk turned to Jenny and Daniel. 'How's it progressing?' Hedra asked. 'I saw you in the pub the other day and Daniel seemed quite smitten.'

'Well he doesn't have Cador's cheek and in fact is rather serious by nature. We've been dating since before Christmas and as long as I don't frighten him off, I think we'll be fine. Those Holmes boys are fabulous and I'm mad about him. If I play my cards right, I could be Zelda's sister-in-law.'

Zelda smiled over her shoulder at her, 'I like the sound of that.' she said.

'So Hedra are you helping out in the Anchor pub then?' Patti asked.

'Yes, Maisie needed extra help in the bar and until the Agency starts, that solves the cash flow problem.'

They were approaching the village and Zelda dropped Hedra off first then Patti and Jenny. 'Thanks girls that worked out well.' she said, as she kissed each one goodbye.

The wedding was booked at the local church in the village, for the Saturday the week before Easter. That left the venue for the reception still to be decided. Although holding it at the Hall was a possibility, both Cador and Zelda finally agreed, it was less hassle to let other people take the strain.

'Darling you supply all the hotels and restaurants around the area so which one do you think is the best?' Zelda asked.

'Well there is a lovely hotel about three miles from the church. I'm friends with the owners so I'll contact them and we can go over and see what you think.'

'I like the sound of that, let professionals do everything then you and I can just enjoy the day.'

Zelda turned and kissed Cador. It was lovely that he always knew the right way to do things. Why did I think Harrison was worldly and Donald was sophisticated while the one person who can get things done correctly was right under my nose all the time?

'What was that for?' Cador said in mock surprise.

'Just counting my blessings.' Zelda replied. 'By the way, I've sent out all the invitations, if all of them accept there will be well over a hundred guests. Do you think the church will be big enough?'

'Yes, my ancestors built that church and they did things big, so no worries on that score.'

'I've had a reply from Rick in America, he has accepted and will be coming over with his wife. Isn't that nice?'

Cador nodded. 'It gets better and better. As it's taking place here where I was born, I'm afraid it will be my side of the church that will have the most people.'

'Well I've asked several old friends, but it's sad that I don't have any relative to see me married.'

Zelda bit her lip, but then looking up into Cador's dark eyes she felt happy again and said, 'One day I hope we will have our own family.'

'Nothing less than a football team.' he laughed.

'Hang on,' she said, 'I've just gone off the idea.'

'Don't worry darling, we'll just enjoy ourselves first.'

The Swansrock Manor Hotel proved to be just the venue Zelda wanted. It stood in acres of landscaped gardens with a large lake complete with an island and elegant swans swimming lazily around. Surrounding the house were terraces that, as the owner pointed out were just right for taking photographs.

Mario, the French chef took them through the possible menus in a devastating accent. 'Do you want zee three course meal or zee buffet option?' he enquired gazing at Zelda with smouldering eyes. 'You will be zee most jolie bride I have ever cooked for, pardon moi, I mean beautiful bride. I will make everything 'tres bon'.'

'Is this guy for real?' Whispered Cador.

Zelda shushed him. 'Oh I think definitely 'sit down' don't you Cador?'

'Fine by me, you tell Mario what you want and I'll go and talk to Clarisse and Jimmy about the other details.' Standing up Cador kissed Zelda and shook Mario's hand. 'Whatever the lady wants to order Mario, and only the best.' he said walking back to reception.

Zelda did just that. The meal would be one that their guests would enjoy and remember.

As Mario left the room with many compliments and assurances that he would produce a banquet fit for a Queen, Clarisse came in and took her seat beside Zelda.

'Cador tells me you don't have any relatives. Normally the bride's mother would come up with opinions and suggestions. It's hard to remember everything so would you like me to play that role?'

'Oh please.' A relieved Zelda said. 'I was just starting to panic.'

'Don't worry, let's agree a date and you can come here and we'll go through everything. Jimmy and I are very fond of Cador, It's about time he settled down.'

Zelda smiled, 'I never thought when I first met him that we would end up together, but I'm over the moon and I want our wedding to be perfect.'

Clarisse squeezed her hand. 'Trust me it will be.'

Driving back Zelda gazed at Cador's strong hands on the steering wheel and sighed happily. 'Darling you do spoil me.'

'Why not?' he said, 'besides I enjoy it.'

'We'll exchange rings at the ceremony. I'd like to see you with a big gold wedding ring, you have really nice hands.'

Cador laughed, 'You mean for a man of the soil.'

'No, you know I didn't mean that, but I'm serious, what do you think?'

'Yes, it's a lovely idea, we'll go shopping for them together.'

'What about your Stag night?' Zelda queried.

'I've decided to have a couple of days with Daniel and some of my surfing buddies in Newquay. I'll arrange a Hen Night for you and whoever you want to spend it with, and then a pamper day at the new Spa hotel. I reckon the best time would be just before the wedding. How does that grab you?'

'Brilliant.' Zelda said. 'I think my three bridesmaids would be all I want.'

'OK, leave it to me.'

They had arrived back at Marryat House and Cador dropped Zelda off, then drove on to Hawke Hall to see Daniel and make arrangements for his surfing Stag jaunt.

The days whizzed by in a flurry of plans for the wedding. Clarisse thought of everything. Seating plans, place names, table decorations, colour schemes, choice of wines, flowers, music, wedding cars; the list was endless. 'You are marvellous,' Zelda said at one of their many meetings.

'I've overseen more weddings than I've had hot dinners', Clarisse smiled, 'you'd be surprised, if I didn't jog memories how many marriages would be over before they had even started.'

On the day of Zelda's Hen night, a big white stretch limousine arrived outside the house. Dressed in a short white dress and veil with a large L sign on her back Zelda led the giggling girls out, each with their overnight bag. They drove past the Anchor pub to the waves and cheers from the regulars lined up outside. The landlord having been tipped off by Cador. Then onto a restaurant in Truro for a slap up meal, followed by a visit to a club where they danced until midnight. Slightly merry and hot after their exertions on the dance floor, they piled into the waiting limo and were whisked away to the Spa hotel.

Next day after a leisurely swim, they opted for massages, facials and whatever took their fancy, including a healthy lunch.

'My word,' Jenny said, 'our Cador knows how to lay on a wonderful treat. After yesterday's wild night I needed this.'

'I felt about a hundred this morning.' Her sister chimed in.

'And looked it.' Jenny agreed as Patti threw a towel at her.

'Now girls no fighting.' Zelda said as well as she could, due to the drying facemask the beautician had just applied.

Hedra padded up proudly showing off her cyclamen pink toed feet having had her first ever pedicure. They had all agreed to have their nails painted the same shade, which was a deeper colour pink than their bridesmaid dresses.

Late in the afternoon Cador arrived to take them home.

'Thank you that was fun.' The girls chorused and kissed him before climbing into his four by four.

'Well I must say you all look wonderful.' Cador said, as they filed past him.

Zelda got a lingering kiss from him to a chorus of whistles and cries of 'Find a room.'

During the drive back they excitedly told him all the details of the trip and about the beauty treatments they had enjoyed.

'This feels like picking up children on a school run,' he laughed adding, 'I've taken Henry up to Hawke Hall like you suggested Zelda. Daniel will look after him until we are back from our honeymoon.'

'Was Henry all right about that?' A worried Zelda asked.

'Henry was fine, he loves Daniel and he has lots of new places to explore.'

'I'll pop in tonight to see Henry.' Jenny said.

'And Daniel.' They all chorused to much laughter.

The day of the wedding Zelda woke early and lay in bed dozily coming round. At the back of her mind, something said today is special. Then when it dawned on her what it was, she sat up panicking and looked at the clock. It said half past five. Going downstairs to make herself a cup of tea, she missed Henry running up and wagging his tail. Sitting in the kitchen with her tea, she started to run through the things she had to do, but then realised until the hairdresser and make- up artist arrived there was nothing.

Looking round her comfortable kitchen Zelda thought, I wonder if Tommy was still alive, what he would have made of today. His only daughter marrying a man that she would never have met, if it were not for the fatal accident that lead to her inheriting the house. However, as Americans say 'what goes around comes around' and Tommy, if you are looking down, I really do think we will be happy. Her tea finished, and now feeling wide-awake, Zelda went upstairs and had a shower.

Everyone arrived at ten o'clock, Bedlam reigned. The man taking the video was getting in the way of the photographer taking still photos, who was impeding the make-up girl, who was tripping over the lead of the hairdresser's straightening tongs. 'We have an annexe and several rooms, let's spread out a bit.' Zelda said eventually, and some order returned.

Finally, Jenny, Patti and Hedra lined up in their bridesmaid's dresses for Zelda to see. With their real rosebud circular coronets and matching bouquets, they stood smiling at her.

'You look lovely,' she said, 'and Cador asked me to give you these, and you are to wear them today.' She handed each one a case containing an amethyst and silver necklace, then helped them to fasten the clasps.

'Wonderful.' Hedra said excitedly gazing at herself in the mirror. 'I've never had anything as gorgeous as this.'

Standing back to look at her three bridesmaids Zelda smiled. 'You all look a picture and the necklaces are the icing on the cake.'

The car that was to take them to the church arrived and in a flurry of floating chiffon, they ran out leaving just a fragrant whiff of French perfume behind them.

Karen arrived, resplendent in a gold satin suit and enormous dark blue hat, and after dropping Miles off, drove on to the church.

The hairdresser was just fixing Zelda's tiara and veil. 'I'll be down in a minute.' Zelda called out and when she did glide down the stairs to the hall, Miles felt his throat tighten.

'My dear you look lovely, Cador is a very fortunate man. Now have you got everything? The car is waiting outside'

'Ready as I'll ever be.' She said breathlessly taking his arm.

The assembled helpers waved them off, saying Zelda was one of the loveliest brides they had ever seen and promising to lock the house up when they had finished the snacks and drinks she had left out for them.

After they arrived at the church door Jenny, as chief bridesmaid fussed with Zelda's veil and train. As they stood there, a worried looking usher called Tom approached.

'A man I didn't recognise came up and said he didn't have an invitation, but could he come to the reception after the service. He said he didn't think you would mind.'

Zelda felt a stab of apprehension. Things had been going too smoothly. Her fear was it could be Donald about to make trouble. 'Did you get a name?' She queried.

Tom shook his head. 'No he moved inside too quickly, I didn't have time.'

'OK, we must go in now, but thanks Tom. Ready everyone? Here we go.'

With Zelda holding Miles's arm leading, and the three Bridesmaids taking up the rear, they entered the church to the strains of the Wedding March. Cador and Daniel, resplendent in their grey Morning suits, turned to look as Zelda approached.

'You are a lucky guy.' Daniel muttered feeling in his jacket pocket to check the ring was still there.

'The luckiest ever.' Cador said and held out his hand as Zelda reached him with a dazzling smile.

All through the service, Zelda couldn't forget that somewhere in the congregation there was an uninvited person. However, nothing untoward did happen. They exchanged their vows in strong voices that echoed round the church, and then slipped the gold wedding rings on one another's fingers. With the choir singing, Zelda and Cador made their way back up the aisle past the rows of smiling faces.

In the car on the way to the reception Zelda told Cador about the mystery man that wanted to be a guest.

'Don't let it spoil our day, darling.' Cador said. 'Whatever happens I'm here and will sort it out. Don't forget you have a pack of big surfers among the guests, they can tackle anything.'

Zelda nodded and kissed him. 'You are right, it's most likely nothing. Here we are at Swansrock Manor, let's dash in and grab a glass of Champagne before everyone gets here.'

'That's my girl.' Cador laughed, 'get your priorities right.'

The guests filed in past waitresses holding trays of Champagne. At the entrance to the reception area Zelda and Cador stood together smiling, while everyone wished them good luck and a long and happy married life. The final person in the line was a man Zelda had never seen before. His complexion was that of someone who had spent a lot of time in the sun. The white hair was thick and he smiled readily. When he reached Zelda, he stared at her with a long searching gaze.

'Hello my dear Zelda. I read the announcement of your forthcoming marriage in the Times newspaper, I just had to come and see you tie the knot.'

Zelda still could not make any connection to this charming elderly man. 'I'm sorry not to recognise you, so how do you know me?'

'I am Eddie your grandfather, I was the first husband of Grace, your grandmother and Margarita, your mother was our daughter.'

'I thought you were....' Zelda's voice trailed away.

'Dead?' Eddie finished her sentence with a chuckle. 'Yes everyone wrote me off. However, as you can see I am here and very much alive. A property developer, who wanted to build a hotel on the site of my bar and cafe in Spain, made me an offer I couldn't refuse. I bought a lovely little Mews cottage just off the Kings Road with the proceeds.'

Cador held out his hand. 'Well this is a big surprise Eddie, Zelda was only recently saying that she didn't have any relatives to see her married and here you are. When we get back from honeymoon, you must come and stay with us and then you and Zelda can catch up properly. I will include you in my speech, it will be a showstopper.'

Zelda smiled at them both. 'This is the happiest day of my life and it has just been made even happier.'

And the three of them went in to take their places at the top table to applause from the waiting guests.

# CHAPTER 19
# SURPRISING CHANGES

The honeymoon was all that Zelda had expected and more. When they were visiting the Italian towns and beaches, Cador was like a small boy enjoying discovering the places he had only read about. However, in other ways when back at the hotels he was like a very old and experienced boy, he certainly knew his way around a bedroom. The Italian cuisine at the many restaurants they visited gave him a completely new slant on food.

'I knew there was more to pasta than just tinned spaghetti, but this is phenomenal.' He said, as he enjoyed Spaghetti Tetrazzini in a friendly, buzzing restaurant.

Zelda smiled happily at him over a plate of Risotto au frutti di mare. 'In Cornwall I'm the one with L plates on, but out here I can open your eyes to new horizons, It works well.'

All too soon, the weeks had passed and they were aboard the plane on their way back, suntanned and quite a few pounds heavier.

'Are you OK Princess? You're very quiet.' Cador said, taking her hand, a concerned look on his face.

Zelda nodded, 'Yes I'm fine but I have a nagging thought that won't go away. Remember you said if I ever wanted to open a restaurant, I could use the old barn at the harbour? Well I would like to make it into an Italian Bistro, serving lovely food just as we have been enjoying on holiday. I feel I have room for one more shot at a business before we try for your football team, what do you think?'

Cador thought for a while. 'Hmm, that could be a runner. With the guys I used to renovate Hawke Hall to tart up the barn, and also I'll ask Clarisse and Jimmy to recommend the best people to design the interior and install a professional kitchen. That should keep you quiet for a bit, and I believe it could do well. Look at all the punters that came to your teashop. Have you a name in mind?'

'Yes, what do think about The Boat Barn Bistro? It rather says what it is and what it does'.

'That sounds good to me. So shortly, we could be in the Good Food Guide, what a multi tasker you are, hardly any time left for me.'

Zelda bent over as far as her seatbelt would allow as they were just coming in to land and kissed his cheek. 'Silly boy, you know you come first in everything I do.' Her words stopped as the pilot put the plane's engine into reverse thrust and they were back in England.

Arriving at Hawke Hall the door was opened by an excited line up of Patti, Hedra and Daniel.

'Carry her over the threshold.' They chorused.

'OK Mrs Holmes, I hope you are ready for this.' Cador said scooping Zelda up as if she was a feather and stepping into the cool hall to cheers from all.

Henry was barking and his tail was wagging furiously, glad to see them home.

'My, what a welcome.' Zelda said. 'Gosh I have missed you all. However, we have had a fabulous time.'

'Who is for a cup of tea?' Patti asked, heading for the kitchen. 'I'll put the kettle on then it is all yours.'

As they sat sipping their tea and after a round up of all that had gone on since Zelda and Cador had been away, Patti handed Zelda a Newspaper. 'Have a read of that.' She said, implying that it was startling news.  Zelda read the headlines and her hand flew to her chest like a Victorian heroine in a mystery play.  The large letters at the top of the front page read;

"Award Winning Media Director Missing"

"The search by Coastguards for Harrison de Ville continues after his bloodstained car was discovered abandoned at the top of Beachy Head, the beauty spot in Sussex. His distraught wife Giselle told reporters that Mr de Ville attacked her when they were in bed following an argument over their Media Company and then he drove away in his car. This is her second tragedy in a week, as her father died suddenly of a heart attack only a couple of days before.  Sussex police are investigating and will hold a news conference later today."

Zelda shook her head as she came to the end of the article, and then looked at the date. 'This is over two weeks ago; I cannot imagine Harrison attacking her; it's just not like him.  Have there been any developments since?'

'Only that police are questioning Giselle, who is singing like a bird about how awful Harrison was and that he was trying to take away her Inheritance of the media company, and that he was a womaniser.'

'Poppycock, Harrison stopped the divorce to get control of the media company as that was their bargaining demand, it sounds like she and her father reneged on the deal. Is there any more news, have they found a body yet?'

Patti came over and put an arm round Zelda as she could see the stricken look on her face. 'No, they had helicopters and boats searching the beaches and coast and flying all the way to France, but nothing has turned up so far. I'm sorry to give you the bad news after your wonderful honeymoon but it's best you know now as you will find out the minute you put the TV on. It's headline news still.'

Cador had been listening intently. 'I can't believe Harrison would attack anyone, whatever the provocation. It's not in his nature. Remember at the barbeque he was on the receiving end of Donald's fist. It sounds like this Giselle is covering up the truth.'

Zelda looked a bit more cheerful and gazed adoringly at him saying. 'Yes, I refuse to think Harrison is dead, until they find a body there is hope.'

'On a more upbeat topic,' Patti said, 'the holiday letting business is really starting to take off. Word has circulated and even before our ad campaign has started, the phone has been ringing with owners wanting us to put their property on our books.'

'That's great!' Zelda smiled at her, glad of some good news at last. 'Have you found a firm to do the cleaning and washing for the weekly or fortnightly change overs?'

'There's a lovely mother and daughter who have a cleaning firm in the village, and jumped at the chance to do that for us.'

'Well done,' Zelda said, 'you obviously don't need me to help, which is great. I'll have to move my stuff up here from Marryat House, so I'll be busy in the next few days.'

The next day Zelda was amazed at how many trips it took in the car to bring all her personal possessions the short way up to Hawke Hall.

'I've only been in Cornwall about a year and a half but I've acquired all manner of things.' she confided to Hedra as she met her at the front door.

'Luckily the Hall has lots of space so that will not be a problem.' Hedra said, picking up a couple of jumpers that had leapt from the pile that Zelda was carrying.

Up in the Master bedroom Zelda looked round with a fond smile at the scene of her first night with Cador after he proposed. The well-known interior designer, that the builder used, was thrilled at the age of the Hall. He had just completed fitting out a Turkish Hotel for a Russian Billionaire, therefore the theme he used was extravagant and reminiscent of old Russia. Zelda actually loved it and called it "The Catherine the Great Suite." The huge bed had a large red satin panel on the wall behind it that matched the red and gold satin covers. Either side of the bed were long gold edged mirrors with gold shaded lights suspended in front of them, giving plenty of reflected light. To the left of the bed was a row of mirror-fronted closets, and on the right, a massive bathroom. This was where the designer had excelled himself. Under a large round, suspended opaque false ceiling, there twinkled many tiny lights. Beneath it was a large round whirlpool bath. The walls were covered in Italian white grained marble and many backlit mirrors. Black marble covered all surfaces and all fitments were gold plated. An opaque door hid the double shower. A door besides the one leading to the bathroom revealed a dressing room containing several built in sliding doors that hid more hanging space, shelves and drawers. Like many of the bedrooms, it contained a chaise longue and a period writing desk. Either side of the long window, looking out to the sea, were a pair of upholstered tub chairs. In the few quiet moments Zelda could snatch, she would love to sit there and gaze out at the ever-changing seascape, sometimes stormy, sometimes the waves sunlit and calm.

Everything finally stowed away, it was getting dark and Zelda was downstairs in the kitchen when she heard the back door open. 'Is that you Cador?' she called out.

Then she noticed Henry was rigid and tense. A tall figure stumbled out of the dark corridor from the back door and into the kitchen. Henry bounded forward growling, Zelda stifled a scream. The figure looked like a tramp who had spent many nights sleeping rough. His matted hair was partly covered by the hood of a filthy tracksuit; it could have once been grey, but it was hard to tell. His face was covered by many days of stubble, not tidy enough to call a beard. As Henry reached the man, he stopped and then licked the dirty hand the man held out. Zelda moved forward, something about this terrifying figure struck a chord, the eyes looked at her. Even though they were sunken and bloodshot, she recognized the intense blue.

'Harrison! My God, you are alive.' she gasped. 'You poor thing, come in and sit down. Now before you say anything let me get you a cup of tea.'

The figure limped in and collapsed on to a chair by the kitchen table his chin slumped on his chest, while Zelda made a very strong mug of tea with several spoons of sugar in it. Harrison took it and downed it in one gulp. 'Thanks.' he muttered. His once lovely voice, dry and gravelly.

'Harrison, before I start asking you about where you have been, are you hurt?'

Without a word, Harrison pulled back the hood of the tracksuit disclosing a deep wound covered in dried blood and matted hair. Zelda immediately picked up her mobile phone and called Jenny.

'Jenny can you come up to the Hall now?' She said when Jenny answered. 'It is an emergency, and can you bring your bag of tricks. I have a patient for you?'

'On my way, be with you in five.' Jenny answered.

When she arrived, Jenny, always the cool professional, took one look at Harrison and turning to Zelda said.

'First we must give Harrison a bath and wash his hair, and then we can see what the damage is.'

'OK, use the downstairs bathroom. Now Harrison you go with Jenny, I'll go and find some of Cador's things and bring them down.'

Then she whispered to Jenny to put his old clothes outside the door of the bathroom and that she would dispose of them. As Jenny helped Harrison out of the kitchen, Zelda smiled as she heard her say, 'Don't worry Harrison I'm not going to see anything that I don't see every day of the week.'

At that moment, Cador arrived. 'Darling, a big surprise. Harrison has turned up, he's in a bad way but Jenny is with him and assessing the damage. What he needs is new clothes, as I'm throwing away his old ones. Can you get him one of your T Shirts, a pair of underpants and some jogging bottoms, oh! and a pair of slippers, and then with a bit of food inside him we can ask Harrison what happened.'

As she collected the heap of filthy clothes and took them outside to the bins, she looked sadly at the shoes Harrison had just taken off. They had once been very expensive slip on boat shoes, but now the leather uppers had come away from the soles and there was blood on the heels, no doubt from blisters. How many hundreds of miles must he have walked, and what prompted him to arrive here in Cornwall? She returned to the kitchen and carried on preparing the meal.

When Harrison and Jenny emerged from the bathroom, Harrison was just recognisable, but painfully thin and drawn. Jenny had cut, or more correctly hacked off most of his hair and a large white bandage covered the gash on his temple and into his hairline.

'Sit down everyone.' Zelda said, placing large plates of Shepherd's pie and green beans in front of them.

'This is lovely, darling.' Cador said as they tucked in.

'Well the beans from your market garden couldn't be fresher.' Zelda said. 'That's the secret to beans, they are best eaten the day they are picked.'

She realised this was a ludicrous conversation as they tried to appear normal so that Harrison had a chance to eat his meal before they fired questions at him. He had cleared his plate and then Zelda produced a large apple crumble and a jug of custard. In times of stress, comfort food was the best answer she thought, noting that Harrison was less trancelike than when he arrived. Henry was sitting with his chin on Harrison's knee and for once, she didn't tell Henry to go to his bed.

'Coffee in the sitting room?' Cador said, 'I'll get it and bring it in.'

When they were all sitting ranged around on the large sofas in the cavernous sitting room, Zelda smiled at Harrison and quietly said, 'Can you remember what happened and how you came to be here?'

There was a long pause and it was obvious Harrison was dredging up what he could from his fuzzy recollections. 'I remember being in bed with Giselle at our house near Eastbourne, and her continuing the argument we had been having about the media business. She said that as her father had died before he had made the business over to me, it would remain hers. When I said that if that were the case I would resume divorce proceedings, I felt this tremendous blow on the head. I could feel the blood pouring down my face, but managed to put the light on. Giselle had the small marble bedside clock in her hand, the glass face had smashed and there was hair and skin all over it and her hand.'

Jenny and Zelda's faces were frozen in horror.

'Oh Harrison, that is horrible but do go on if you can.' Zelda said, trying to keep her voice steady.

'I stumbled to the car, which I had left outside and drove away. I'm glad it was night as I kept nearly passing out. I must have passed out completely, because when I came round it was light and realised the car was on the edge of a cliff. There was blood all over me and the car. I took off my bloodstained T-shirt and pants. On the back seat was all my sports gear so I changed into that before passing out again. People were walking their dogs but it was very misty so I left the car and started walking. I can't remember where or for how long, it was light and then it was dark, no one noticed me. I was cold and I was hungry. Eventually, after what must have been days, I came across a group of homeless people. They were under a bridge, which is where they lived. They looked after me and didn't ask questions. A local supermarket gave them food that had passed its sell by date and then they barbequed it in a shopping trolley. I don't know how long I was with them, but eventually I said I must get on. I didn't know where I was, or where I was heading but for some reason I came here. I tried your house first Zelda and then I came to where I could see lights. Why are you here?'

'You have a lot to catch up with.' Zelda said leaning forward. 'Cador and I are now married. It was a lovely wedding and I'm very happy. We now own Hawke Hall, and were away on our honeymoon when all your drama happened, so we have only just caught up.'

Harrison looked at Cador and for the first time since he arrived smiled.

'Congratulation, you never gave up did you?'

'If you really want something that's what you do.' Cador said holding Zelda's hand.

'We'll have to tell the police you're safe,' Zelda said quietly. 'They have been searching for you, and Giselle has been all over the media claiming you attacked her.'

'The bitch.' Harrison muttered.

'Exactly, however, don't worry. When she came to see me at the teashop, and I thought she was going to be a complaining customer, I recorded our conversation. A tip I picked up when I worked as Donald's PA. So I have her saying that her father was signing the business over to you if you stopped the divorce proceedings.'

'How did she not know you were recording her?'

'I had the recorder hidden amongst a load of menus and leaflets I was carrying, and she was so busy thinking she was giving me a hard time that she didn't notice.'

'That was clever.' Said Jenny. 'But Harrison, I'll tell the police, you should go to the hospital to have a complete check-up. Your head should have had stitches all those weeks ago, but a surgeon needs to assess what to do now.'

'Tonight you can sleep here and we'll leave it until the morning to call the police. It's important that you get a good night's sleep before all the questioning starts.' Zelda said getting up from the sofa.

'Thank you, I don't feel ready to face that yet.' A heavy eyed Harrison started to get up from his seat and gratefully accepted Cador's' helping hand.

'I've put you in the Turret room, it's nice and quiet up there and it has its own en-suite. Do you think you can make it up the stairs?' Zelda said, leading the way with Jenny bringing up the rear clutching a pack of pills to administer before they left Harrison tucked up for the night.

When Zelda and Jenny joined Cador downstairs, he had a gin and tonic ready for them. 'What an evening.' he said, 'I thought we needed this.'

'Cheers!' they said, gratefully sipping the rather stiff concoction, and sinking back into the soft cushions.

'It will be a hell of a day tomorrow once the police descend here.' Jenny said, 'So I'll phone the Surgery and tell them I'll be in when I can, they will just have to manage. Harrison was lucky not to get blood poisoning, and I still think he's a bit concussed.'

'I wonder if they will charge Giselle with anything. After all she has lied and could be charged with attempted murder.' Zelda said, 'I didn't like her one bit.'

Cador laughed. 'She should have thought twice before tangling with you darling. That was a clever move of yours to record the conversation, It will blow her case that Harrison attacked her sky high.' They chatted some more about the day's happenings and then Cador escorted Jenny home, and Henry got an unexpected walk.

The next morning Harrison didn't emerge until after nine o'clock. 'That was the best night's sleep I have ever had.'

He said, as he walked into the kitchen where Zelda and Cador were both sitting with a cup of tea.

'What do you fancy to eat?' Zelda inquired.

'Can I have a boiled egg please?'

'With soldiers?' Zelda inquired meaning it as a joke. But Harrison's face lit up and he nodded.

'Do you know when I was just walking along in a sort of haze, not knowing where I was, I passed several places with hens clucking about and I really fancied a boiled egg at that moment. I was very hungry.'

'In that case I'll make it two eggs.' Zelda smiled at him and busied herself at the Aga cooker.

'When you've had breakfast, I'll phone the police and let them know you are here.' Cador said, 'You do understand we must tell them, we can't put it off any longer.'

Harrison was feeling his stubbly chin. 'Yes I do realise that. Do you know I quite like my beard? But I suppose I must get rid of it, have you a spare razor Cador?'

Cador laughed. 'Here we are talking about beards when you are the most famous missing person in Britain at this moment. I suppose we could give you designer stubble with a small beard, that would be a rather trendy look.'

Zelda placed the plate with the two eggs in their eggcups in front of Harrison, and the fingers of buttered bread on another plate beside them. As he tucked in Jenny arrived and Cador left the room to phone the police from his study.

'Hello,' Jenny said, 'I see the patient has a hearty appetite.'

Yes, I'm feeling much better.' Harrison said, starting on his second egg. 'Thanks to the wonderful treatment I received last night.'

'Have you thought what you will do once all this is sorted out?' Zelda said, pouring Jenny and Harrison a cup of tea. 'Will you fight Giselle for the media company?'

Harrison thought for a long time, then his face took on a look of sudden realisation. 'No,' he said, 'I will let Giselle have it. I was the driving force there and without me, it will fold in six months, besides I don't want anything to do with her anymore. I could start my own media company, but what I really want to do after this experience, is to work for a charity helping homeless people. Those guys who looked after me were super chaps and their tales were a real eye opener. Some were homeless because of bad divorces where they had lost everything, others had owned businesses that had failed, or for some of them it was just bad luck. With my media background, I could really help and it would be most fulfilling. I've had an easy time up to now, but everything happens for a reason.'

'Well don't rush into anything,' Jenny said, 'you've had quite a medical trauma and you need time to get over it.'

Cador came in with an electric razor in his hand. 'Let's see if we can give you a less barbaric look before the police arrive. They said they would be here in about twenty minutes.'

When the two police officers arrived, a much more presentable Harrison was waiting in the kitchen with a small neat beard and designer stubble. His large bandage gave him quite a rakish look. After the initial questions about how he came to be at Hawke Hall and why he hadn't made contact with anyone, Jenny intervened.

'Following that heavy blow to his head, I believe Harrison suffered concussion and is still, in my professional opinion quite unwell. What he needs is to go immediately to a local hospital before we waste any more time. I'm a trained nurse so I know what I'm talking about.'

The police officer who was taking down details, shut his note pad and looked in awe at Jenny. Pretty and tough, just how he liked women. 'We'll take Harrison to Truro hospital right away. He'll be quite OK there; as I'm sure, when the press get wind that he's been found they'll be down here like a swarm of bees.'

'Thanks for everything, you have all been wonderful.' Harrison said as he was helped into the back seat of the police car.

'I'll come back and take statements from you all in a few days' time and let you know how Harrison is getting on.' the policeman said, as Harrison gave a weak wave through the car window, and was whisked away in the arms of the law.

'Well that was a snappy outcome. Jenny you are one fierce lady when being medical.' Cador said. 'But that was what was needed, Harrison is in quite a bad way.'

'They can ask him what they like after he's had that head attended to and a brain scan. I'm sure he is going to be fine eventually, but he doesn't need hassle right now.' Cador kissed them both goodbye.

'I have to meet a man at the barn site, things are progressing and there are men working all over it. I'll be back for a quick snack at lunchtime, see you then Zelda.' He drove off with the ever-faithful Henry looking out of the front seat window, ears flying in the breeze.

'And I'd better get off to the Surgery.' Jenny said. 'keep me posted with developments.'

Zelda wandered back to the house and switched on the television news programme. There were live pictures of Giselle being arrested and taken to a police station. The running strip at the bottom of the screen read; "Giselle de Ville has been charged with attempted murder following forensic tests on blood found at the scene of the crime. These proved to be only that of her husband Harrison".

When Cador returned just after midday, Zelda couldn't wait to tell him the news, running excitedly to meet him. 'They have arrested Giselle.' she blurted out as he got out of the car, Henry jumping out, his tail wagging nineteen to the dozen.

'That's great.' Cador said, standing with a grin on his face.

'What is it darling?' Zelda said,

'Remember I said when Prince died that I nearly bought you a puppy but didn't as you were so busy? Well I now know we are never going to have a quiet time so....'

With that, he pulled down the zip of his jacket and a little furry head struggled out. Zelda screamed with delight and ran forward.

'It's a girl,' Cador said, 'I thought Henry would accept that better. She has a really long pedigree, and is an Irish Red Setter just like Henry, but I think she will be a darker shade of red than him.'

Zelda held her hands out and Cador put the tiny warm, wriggly puppy in them. 'Oh darling she is beautiful. You are the loveliest man in the world, shall we call her Rusty?'

**END**

# THANK YOU
# FOR READING

If you enjoyed this book, keep your eyes peeled for Amanda's next novel: THE HUMTONS. A satirical tale of two villages and their inhabitants.

## EXTRACT FROM THE HUMPTONS
## THE LOCAL AUTUMN SHOW

Madge placed the wicker basket containing the washed and perfectly shaped carrots into the boot of her mud spattered car, then stood back to gaze with pride at the pick of her crop.

'Beat that Jimmy Griggs.' she muttered. Then slamming down the tailgate she drove to the village hall going over the humpbacked bridge that separated Little Humpton from Greater Humpton. The rivalry between the two villages was intense and none more so than when the inhabitants took part in the Autumn Show.

Meanwhile Daisy Biggers was carefully unpacking her scrumptious looking cupcakes on to a trestle table that was covered with a white tablecloth. She found a space between Miranda Fowler's rather soggy efforts and Fanny Jones suspiciously shop-bought looking entry. Whenever the village cricket team's members wives took their cakes and sandwiches for the cricketer's afternoon tea it was always Fanny's sad looking efforts that were left untouched. Although young and pretty, she was also quite shy and retiring.  Her rejected culinary offerings did nothing for her self-esteem.

'Good morning everyone' Madge breezed, 'What time are we expecting our Judges?'

'They said they will arrive promptly at eleven and they are old school so never late.'  Keith Fowler, the Chairman of Humpton's Horticultural Society replied.

Daisy Biggers smiled as she put her name card against her plate of cakes, making sure Keith saw where they were on the table and would hopefully direct the Judges to them.  Daisy had won best cake Rosette for the last two years and was hoping to make it three in a row.  Yes, a hat trick would be what she deserved.

Madge propped her name card up on her neatly arranged three carrots, the stipulated number.  Glancing at Jimmy's three carrots, she noted that they were definitely of an inferior size and shape.  As neighbours, they had battled for years over the 'Best Vegetable' category and this year Madge had spent months weeding out her rows of carrots until she had three perfect specimens.  Her carrots stood out among the withered and lumpy beetroots and onions that had seen better day.

There was a scrunch on the gravel outside as Sir Jolyon and Lady Phyllis Chudleigh arrived in their Rolls, driven by Busby their chief steward and man of many parts.

A flustered Keith Fowler rushed forward to welcome them, but in his eagerness tripped and fell forward into the large bosom of Lady Phyllis.  He regained his composure after untangling himself from her ladyships cleavage but managed to get her diamond brooch stuck in what little remained of his hair.

'On behalf of Little Humptons Autumn Show may I...' Keith began however, by then a harrumphing Sir Jolyon was already inside the Hall followed by a distinctly flushed Lady Phyllis prodding her ebony walking stick into anyone in her path.

Miranda already had her heavily bejewelled hand on Sir Jolyon's arm and was steering him over to the cake table.

'These are the cakes made by the ladies of the village.' she said in her breathless, little girl voice. 'The names are on them.' she continued indicating her own name by the worst looking plate of cakes.'

Keith and Lady Phyllis joined them 'We don't have to eat them, do we? Lady Phyllis queried quite horrified at the thought.

'Only a small amount' said Keith, smoothing his hair and handing the diamond brooch back to Lady Phyllis, who after giving him a withering look, pinned it back on her ample chest.

Sir Jolyon was already on the other side of the Hall where the vegetables were displayed.

'Not as good as those in my walled kitchen garden.' He remarked.

Madge bristled saying. 'But you have a gardener we grow them ourselves in our back gardens.'

Lady Phyllis joined them. 'Quite right, you tell him,' she boomed adding 'which are yours, my dear?'

Madge indicated her plate then gasped. The names had been switched and Jimmy Griggs name was beside her plate.

'Someone is cheating.' She exclaimed and switched the names back.

'You can't do that!' Jimmy shouted.

'I just have.' Madge replied.

'This is too much' said Lady Phyllis and followed Sir Jolyon and Miranda into the refreshment tent just in time to see him pinch Miranda, who squealed and Lady Phyllis said witheringly, 'I saw that Jolyon, I have a headache I think I wish to leave.'

It was a command and not one to be ignored.

As they made their way to the exit passing Madge, Sir Jolyon held her hand up.

'The winner of the vegetable class' he said. Then looking round spotted a downcast looking Fanny, 'and this lady is the winner of the cakes, well done.'

With that, the Judges climbed into the Rolls and as they were whisked away, Lady Phyllis could be seen giving Sir Jolyon a piece of her mind.

'What a shambles' Jimmy Griggs remarked, staring sadly at his second class carrots.

'That should teach you not to try and cheat,' Madge said, as she picked up her plate of carrots with the winners rosette, then swept out to her car.

'Just accepted strategic manoeuvres as practiced on the battlefield.' Jimmy shouted after her. He had been in the army before retiring and his life was still run on army lines.

This year not a single member of Greater Humpton Village received even a runner's up mention.

'Quite understandable,' said Thomas Perkins defensibly, he was the Chairman of their Horticultural Society, 'we get more rain on our side of the river than the Little Humpton lot.'

'What tosh,' fumed Jimmy Griggs, 'you will not just admit our members in Little Humpton produce better exhibits.'

'Well my carrots were waterlogged for months' Thomas replied.

'Drainage, my dear chap, drainage.' said Jimmy, 'get your troops ready for next weeks Knotted String battle, we may win that as well.'

Jimmy had been quite "top brass" in the Army and while his carrots were not up to scratch, he shone in the local re-enactment tournaments.

'I am running the show for Little Humpton again,' he said, 'my past military experience will come in very handy, though of course on a much smaller and less bloody scale.'

'The American tenant of Foxley Grange, Charles Edward McCreasey is our man for Greater Humpton this time. I feel I must not hog the limelight.' Thomas replied modestly, as Phoebe his wife joined him and they left quickly bearing their rather pathetic looking entries.

Miranda threw her soggy cakes in the rubbish bin and ignored Keith's efforts to placate her. It would take a nice piece of jewellery and a long Cruise to put him back in her good books.

A flushed and beaming Fanny packed the shop bought cakes into her carrier bag and pinned her winner's rosette onto the handle.

'Well that was a success,' Chairman Keith said, 'roll on next year.'

**END**

If you would like to receive an email reminder when THE HUMPTONS is on sale, please send your name and the book title to admin@theendlessbookcase.com, and we will contact you on its release date.